ORPHANS OF ELDORADO

Milton Hatoum was born in Manaus in 1952. His first novel, *Tale of a Certain Orient*, was published in Brazil in 1989 – it was followed by *The Brothers* in 2000 and by *Ashes of the Amazon* in 2005. All three won the prestigious Jabuti Prize for fiction and have been translated into English. The last was awarded the Portugal Telecom Prize for Literature as well. Milton Hatoum also published a collection of short stories in 2009, *A cidade ilhada* (The Island City).

ORPHANS
OF
ELDORADO

milton hatoum

Translated from the Portuguese by
JOHN GLEDSON

CANONGATE
Edinburgh · London · New York · Melbourne

Published by Canongate Books in 2010

I

First published in Brazil in 2008 by Companhia das Letras, Editora Schwarcz Ltda, Rua Bandeira Paulista 702 cj. 32, 04532-002 São Paulo

First published in Great Britain in 2010 by Canongate Books Ltd, 14 High Street, Edinburgh EHI ITE

www.meetatthegate.com

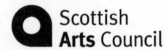

Scottish Arts Council

The publishers gratefully acknowledge subsidy from the Scottish Arts Council towards the English translation of this book

British Library Cataloguing-in-Publication Data
A catalogue record for this book is available on request from the British Library

ISBN 978 1 84767 300 8

Typeset in Centaur MT by Palimpsest Book Production Ltd, Grangemouth, Stirlingshire

Printed and bound in the UK by CPI Mackays, Chatham ME5 8TD

This book is printed on FSC certified paper

Mixed Sources
Product group from well-managed forests and other controlled sources
www.fsc.org Cert no. TT-COC-002341
© 1996 Forest Stewardship Council

To my mother

Myths are universal and timeless stories that reflect and shape our lives—they explore our desires, our fears, our longings and provide narratives that remind us what it means to be human. *The Myths* series brings together some of the world's finest writers, each of whom has retold a myth in a contemporary and memorable way. Authors in the series include: Alai, Karen Armstrong, Margaret Atwood, AS Byatt, Michel Faber, David Grossman, Milton Hatoum, Natsuo Kirino, Alexander McCall Smith, Tomás Eloy Martínez, Klas Östergren, Victor Pelevin, Ali Smith, Su Tong, Dubravka Ugrešić, Salley Vickers and Jeanette Winterson.

The City

You said, 'I'll go to another land, I'll go to
    another sea.
I'll find a city better than this one.
My every effort is a written indictment,
and my heart—like someone dead—is buried.
How long will my mind remain in this decaying state?
Wherever I cast my eyes, wherever I look,
I see my life in black ruins here,
where I spent so many years, and ruined and
    wasted them.'

You will not find new lands, you will not find
    other seas.
The city will follow you. You will roam
the same streets. And you will grow old in the same
    neighbourhood,
and your hair will turn white in the same houses.
You will always arrive in this city. Don't hope for
    elsewhere—
there is no ship for you, there is no road.
As you have wasted your life here,
in this small corner, so you have ruined it on the
    whole earth.

C.P. CAVAFY, 1910

The woman's voice attracted so many people, that I escaped from my teacher's house and went down to the edge of the Amazon to see. An Indian woman, one of the city's *tapuias*, was speaking and pointing to the river. I can't remember what designs were painted on her face; their colour I can remember, though: red *urucum* juice. In the humid afternoon, there was a rainbow that looked like a serpent, embracing the sky and the water.

Florita followed after me, and began translating what the woman was saying in the indigenous language; she would interpret some phrases and then go silent, as if unsure of herself. She was having doubts about the words she was translating: or about her own voice. She was saying she'd left her husband because he spent all his time hunting and wandering here and there, leaving her alone in Aldeia. That is, until the day she was seduced by an enchanted being. Now she was going to live with her lover, deep in the river bed. She wanted to live in a better world, without so much suffering and misfortune. She spoke without looking at the porters on the Market ramp, or at the fishermen and the girls from the Carmo College. I remember the girls began to weep and ran away, and only much later did I understand why.

Suddenly the *tapuia* stopped talking and entered the water. Curious bystanders froze, as if spellbound. And all of them saw how she began to swim calmly in the direction of the Island of the Hoatzins. Her body sank into the shining river, and then someone shouted: The madwoman's going to drown herself. The boatmen sailed over to the island, but they didn't find the woman. She'd disappeared. She never came back.

Florita translated the stories I heard when I played with the little Indian children in Aldeia, right on the edge of the town. Strange legends, they were. Listen to this one: it's the story of a man with an enormous cock, so long it crossed the Amazon, went right through Espírito Santo Island and speared a girl in the Mirror of the Moon Lake. Then the cock wound itself round the man's throat, and while he struggled to avoid being strangled, the girl asked, laughing: Now where's that long cock got to?

I remember too the story of a woman who was seduced by a male tapir. Her husband killed the tapir, cut the animal's penis off and hung it up in the doorway of the hut. The woman covered the penis with mud until it was hard and dry; she spoke affectionately to the little thing and caressed it. Then the husband rubbed a lot of pepper onto the clay cock and watched from his hiding place as the woman licked the little thing and sat astride it. They say she jumped and screamed with so much pain, and that her tongue and body burned like fire. The only way out was to dive into the river and become a toad. And the husband went to live by the riverbank, sad and repentant, begging his wife to come back to him.

These were legends that Florita and I heard from the grandparents of the children in Aldeia. They spoke in the *língua geral*, and later Florita repeated the stories at home, in the lonely nights of my childhood.

One strange story frightened me: the one about the severed head—the divided woman. Her body keeps going in search of food in other villages, while her head takes flight and sticks to her husband's shoulder. The man and the head are conjoined for the whole day. Then, at nightfall, when a bird sings and the first star appears in the sky, the woman's body returns and sticks to the head. But, one night, another man robs half the body. The husband doesn't want to live just with his wife's head; he wants all of her. He spends his life looking for the body, sleeping and waking with his wife's head stuck to his shoulder. The head was silent, but alive; it could feel the world with its eyes, and its eyes didn't shrink—they saw everything. It was a head with a heart.

I was nine or ten, and never forgot. Does anyone hear those voices any more? I began to brood over this, for there is a moment when stories become a part of our lives. One of the heads ruined me. The other wounded my heart and my soul, and left me at the edge of this river, suffering, waiting for a miracle. Two women. But isn't a woman's story a man's story too? Before the First World War, who hadn't heard of Arminto Cordovil? Lots of people knew my name, everyone had heard tell of the wealth of my father, Amando, Edílio's son.

See that lad over there riding a tricycle? He sells ice lollies. Whistling, the slyboots. He's going to move slowly over to the shade of that *jatobá*. In the old days, I could have bought the whole box of lollies, and the tricycle too. Now he knows I can't buy anything. Now, just out of spite, he's going to look at me with owlish eyes. Then he gives a false laugh and pedals off, and over by the Carmo Church he shouts: Arminto Cordovil's a madman. Just because I spend my afternoons looking at the river. When I look at the Amazon, my memory takes flight, a voice comes from my mouth and I only stop talking the moment the big bird sings. The tinamou will appear later, with his grey wings, the colour of the sky at dusk. It sings, saying goodbye to the daylight. Then I fall silent and let night enter my life.

Our life never stops going round in circles. In those days I wasn't living in this filthy ruin. The white palace of the Cordovils, now that was a real house. Once I had decided to live with my beloved in the palace, she disappeared off the face of the earth. They said she lived in an enchanted city, but I didn't believe it. What's more, I was in a parlous state, without a penny to my name. No love, no money and, on top of all that, at risk of losing the white palace. And I hadn't my father's obstinacy—nor his cunning either. Amando Cordovil could have swallowed the whole world. He was fearless: a man who laughed at death. Anyway, see here: good fortune falls in your lap, and a gust of wind blows it all away. I eagerly threw the fortune away, taking a blind pleasure in doing so. I wanted to rub out the past and the ill fame of my grandfather Edílio. I never knew that particular Cordovil. They said he never tired, didn't know what laziness was, and worked like a horse in the humid heat of this land. In 1840, at the end of the Cabano War, he planted cocoa in the Boa Vida plantation, a property on the right bank of the Uaicurapá, a few hours from here by boat. But he died before he realised an old dream: the building of the white palace in this town. Amando moved into the house when he married my mother. Then he began to dream of ambitious destinations for his freighters. One day I'm going to compete with the Booth Line and Lloyd Brasileiro, my father would say. I'm going to carry rubber to Le Havre, Liverpool and New York. Another Brazilian who died still waiting for his day of greatness to arrive. In the end, I found out about other things, but let's not get ahead of ourselves.

I'll recount what my memory can reach, slowly and patiently.

I must have been about twenty when Amando took me to Manaus. My father didn't say a word throughout the journey; only when we got off the boat did he utter these two sentences: You're going to live in the Pension Saturno. And you know why.

It was a small, old pension in Instalação da Província Street. I lived in one of the rooms on the ground floor, and used the bathroom next to the basement, where some lads who'd fled from the Young Apprentices' Institute lived. They did odd jobs, working in bakeries and the German brewery; one of them, Juvêncio, jobless and without qualifications, walked around with a machete, and no one meddled with him. When my father was in his office, Florita would escape to the pension to chat with me and do my washing. She didn't like Juvêncio; she was afraid of being stabbed by him. She detested my room at the Saturno too. She'd say: With that prison cell window, you're sure to die of suffocation. Florita was accustomed to the comfort of the house in the Manaus suburbs, and the white palace in Vila Bela. I asked about Amando, but she didn't tell me everything. She said nothing about the firm's new freighter. I had read in the paper that the vessel was in Manaus Harbour. A steamship with wheels on its sides, built by Holtz, the German shipyard. It was a real freighter; the other two were just lighters or barges. I was proud, and showed Florita the paper.

I was going to do a dinner for him, she said. Your father didn't want me to. He's worried about paying for the boat. Or something else.

Florita wanted me to live with her and Amando: the three of us, in the Manaus house. I wanted that too, and she knew it. Here in Vila Bela they told Florita that my father had been happy with my mother at his side. When she died, Amando didn't know what to do with me. To this day I remember the words that destroyed me: Your mother gave birth to you and died. Florita heard these words, hugged me and took me to the bedroom.

A *tapuia* breastfed me. An Indian's milk, or the

milky gum of the *amapá* tree. I don't remember the
face of that nurse, or of any other, for that matter.
It's a dark time; I've no memory of it. Until the
day Amando came into my room with a girl and
said: She's going to look after you. Florita never left
my side, and that's why I missed her so when I was
living in the Saturno.

In Manaus I did nothing—just read in the dining
room, then dozed off in the afternoon heat and
woke in a sweat, thinking of my father. I was waiting
for something, without knowing what it was. My
greatest worry at that time was knowing if the silent
hostility between my father and myself was my fault
or his. I was still young, and thought the punishment for having abused Florita was deserved, and
that I ought to bear the burden of the guilt. I went
to the Ingleses neighbourhood and hung round the
house in the hope of speaking to my father or being
seen by him. I watched the dining-room windows
and imagined Amando looking passionately at my
mother's portrait. I didn't have the courage to knock
at the door, and carried on down the tree-lined

street, looking at the bungalows and chalets with their immense gardens. Once, at night, I saw a man very like Amando on the Boulevard Amazonas. The same gait, the same height, arms by his side and fists clenched. He was walking alongside a woman, and they stopped in front of the Castelhana water tank. I doubted it could be my father when I saw his hands stroke the woman's hair. As I recall it, I think of the legend of the severed head. The man escaped like a rat: he ran into a dark street, pulling the girl along by her arms. The next day I went to the house. I wanted to know if it was really him I'd seen with a woman on the pavement of the Castelhana. He wouldn't let me in or say a word about it. In the doorway, he said:

What you did to Florita was bestial.

He slowly shut the door, as if he wanted to disappear little by little, and for ever.

He spent most of his time in Manaus. He went by tram to the office and worked even when he was asleep, as he himself used to say. But he often came here. My father liked Vila Bela; he had a morbid attachment to his home town. Before I lived in the Saturno, I'd been two or three times to Manaus on holiday. I didn't want to go back to Vila Bela. It was a journey in time, going back a century. Manaus had everything: electric light, telephones, newspapers, cinemas, theatres, opera. Amando only gave me enough change for the tram. Florita took me to the floating harbour and the aviary in the Matriz Square, then we'd walk round the city, looking at the posters for the films at the Alcazar and the Polytheama, going back to the house in the late afternoon. I waited for Amando on the piano stool. It was an anguished wait. I wanted him to hug me and chat with me, or at least look at me, but I was always greeted with the same question: Been for a walk? Then he'd go over to the wall and kiss my mother's photograph.

I thought I was condemned for ever, guilty of my mother's death, when the lawyer Estiliano appeared in the Rua da Instalação for a chat.

He told me I couldn't moulder in a pension for down-and-outs. He knew it was Amando's decision, his way of punishing his lecherous son. But why didn't I study to get into the law faculty? My father would soon change his mind.

Estiliano was Amando's only friend. 'My dear Stelios'—that's what my father called him. This old friendship had begun in places they recalled out loud, as if they were both still young: the beaches of Uaicurapá and Varre Vento, Macuricanã Lake, where they fished together for the last time, before Estiliano travelled to Recife and came back a lawyer, and Amando married my mother. The five-year separation hadn't cooled their friendship. The two of them always met in Manaus and Vila Bela; they looked admiringly at one other, as if they were looking in a mirror; together, they gave the impression that each believed in the other more than he did in himself.

I saw the lawyer with the same white jacket, the same trousers with braces, and an emblem of Justice on his lapel. His hoarse, deep voice intimidated everyone; he was too tall and robust to be discreet, and drank whole bottles of red wine at any hour of the day or night. When he'd drunk a great deal, he'd talk about the bookshops in Paris as if he was there, though he'd never been to France. Wine and literature were Estiliano's pleasures; I don't know where he put, or hid, the desires of the flesh. I know he translated Greek and French poets. And he looked after the legal side of the business. Amando, an austere man, closed his eyes and covered his ears when his friend recited poems in the Avenida restaurant or the bar in Liceu Square. After Florita, Estiliano was the person nearest to me. Right till the last day.

My father would change. Right, then. I spent two years studying in the Municipal Library; at night, in my room, I read the books Estiliano had lent me. The lads in the basement laughed. The gradu-ate from the Saturno. The man of justice. Juvêncio didn't laugh though. He was shy and serious, a lad of few words. I left the pension when I entered the Free University of Manaus. And in the same week Juvêncio too left the Saturno. He went to live on the pavement in front of the High Life Bar, and I above the Cosmopolitan Grocery Store on the Rua Marquês de Santa Cruz. It was a spacious room with a window overlooking the customs and excise offices. In the Cosmopolitan I got to know the city. The heart and the eyes of Manaus are in its docks and along the bank of the Rio Negro. The great port area swarmed with businessmen, fishermen, colliers, dock-workers, peddlers. I got a job in a store run by a Portuguese man, studied in the morning, had my lunch in the Market and spent the afternoon carrying boxes and serving customers. Even with a tiny wage, I informed Estiliano, I was managing to pay the rent for my room.

Amando insisted on paying, said Estiliano. The separation between you is causing him to suffer, but he's too proud to hold out his hand to his son.

I had intended to go by his house to hold out my hand to this proud man, but chance brought the meeting about sooner. One afternoon I had to go to the Escadaria Quay to carry some boxes to the store. Amando was there, with the firm's business manager. This manager imitated everything about my father, down to his gait. He didn't drink because his boss was a teetotaller, and bought clothes in the Mandarim, Amando's favourite shop. But what really irritated me were his eyes—it was as if they were made of glass. The guy never looked at me. And what in my father was authentic, in him became almost comical. I showed the documents for the goods to the excise officer. I was a few yards away from Amando Cordovil. I waited for acknowledgement, but he looked at my apron and didn't say a word to me: he went over to the kiosk in the Market, with the manager behind him like a pet dog. Two days later the storeowner told me a nephew was coming to work with him. He didn't need me any more.

I never knew for certain if I'd been dismissed on my father's orders, but I still hoped to talk to him. I told the owner of the Cosmopolitan that I was out of work, and that the rent would be late. As he had friends in the harbour, I began to work helping passengers embark and disembark. I spent the whole day at the port and had no time for study.

I got no pay, just tips; I was given clothes, hats and second-hand books. I got to know the captain of the *Atahualpa*, the *Re Umberto*, the *Anselm*, the *Rio Amazonas*. I became friendly with Wolf Nickels, of the *La Plata*. These captains worked for Lamport and Holt, the Ligure Brasiliana, the Lloyd Brasileiro, the Booth Line and the Hamburg–South America. Sometimes I accompanied foreign passengers on a canoe trip to the lakes near Manaus; I took them round the centre of the city—they were mad keen to see the Opera House, and couldn't understand how such a grand work of architecture could exist in the middle of the jungle.

I saw the German freighter close to only once, at dawn, after I'd spent the night at a cheap cabaret in the Rua da Independência. I sat on the floating quay and read the word painted in white on the prow: *Eldorado*. So much greed and illusion! Looking at the freighter, I remembered that Amando hated seeing his son consort with the children in Aldeia. We would catch fish with bows and arrows, bathe in the river and run on the beach. When he appeared

at the top of the Fishermen's Steps, I would return
to the white palace. I remembered the contempt and
the silence too. That hurt more than the stories he
told me in the Boa Vida plantation.

At that time the memories came slowly, like drops
of sweat. I struggled to forget, but I couldn't. Even
without knowing it, I wanted to get close to my
father. Nowadays, the memories return intensely.
And they're clearer.

I was getting used to the work on the harbour. I
talked to young people who were going to study in
Recife, Salvador and Rio de Janeiro. Others were
going to Europe. People arrived from many countries, and from every corner of Brazil. The problem
was the poor; the government didn't know what to
do with them. At dawn, the squares were littered
with families sleeping on old newspapers, and that's
where I read news items about my father, in those
crumpled, dirty pages; the most important news
being the competition for a freight line from Manaus
to Liverpool. If Amando won the franchise he would
get assistance from the government to buy another

freighter. Estiliano confirmed this, saying my father would need me. He wanted me to talk to Amando in Vila Bela.

I asked why we shouldn't meet in Manaus.

In Vila Bela your father's far away from his problems. He's in his own house.

Florita's never been back to see me, I said.

That's my friend bearing a grudge. Jealousy. But that'll come to an end soon.

I didn't know if Amando had already fixed something with Estiliano. I wasn't as young as I used to be, but I didn't have the perspicacity or cunning to suspect a father's trap to catch his son. What I did was to throw myself into the nightlife around the port. With the clothes I was given by the passengers, it wasn't hard to win over women from the famous cabarets. I drank for free on board the *La Plata* and worked as a porter and tourist guide. In the Adolpho Lisboa Market, Zé Braseiro's show attracted the tourists at the same time as it appalled them. He was a lad who only had arms and hands—his legs were two stumps of meat. He went around in a little cart pushed by an assistant. On Saturdays, this assistant set up a trapeze in the storehouse by the fish stalls. Zé Braseiro would climb up a rope and swing round the trapeze, put on his display up above, and was greeted with applause. The tourists wept for pity and left money on the cart. Sometimes he repeated the display in São Sebastião Square, in front of the Opera House.

I'd have lived that way for a long time, but the meeting with Amando changed my life. The city had grown unsettled. The traffic in the port had decreased. It wasn't the war in Europe, the First World War. Not yet. I could see people were irritated, indignant. Everything seemed strange and violent. I read my father's outburst in the papers: he complained about absurd taxes, customs dues, the inefficiency of the port, the ballyhoo of our politics.

That's not the only reason Amando's angry, said Estiliano. He's found out you've abandoned your studies and are wandering around, sleeping in the city brothels.

How did he find out?

He knows everything. He'll tell you about it when we meet him.

Isn't it too late for reconciliation?

It's the chance of a lifetime for you. He's getting old, and you're his only son. You must take a boat to Vila Bela before Christmas.

At the beginning of December I went to the house to see Florita. A neighbour told me she and my father had left for Vila Bela. I went into the garden and peered into the parlour through the gaps in the blinds, but I couldn't see my mother's picture on the wall, though the black piano was still in the same place.

While I was looking at the room, I recalled a recital at the house by the pianist Tarazibula Boanerges, to celebrate Amando Cordovil's purchase of the company's second barge. I was about sixteen at the time. During the dinner, Amando embraced a young guest and said: You've got a vocation for politics; you should be a candidate for Mayor of Vila Bela.

The young man, Leontino Byron, asked which party he should stand for.

That's not important, my father answered. Winning's all that matters.

That was one of the few times I saw Amando enthusiastic, and I was even happy when he introduced me to the guests at dinner. One of them, a director of the Manaus Tramway, wanted me to meet his daughter. He pointed at a young girl next to the piano. She was smiling at the keyboard: she had good teeth, beautiful eyes and features, everything was good and beautiful in fact, only she was too pale; her skin was white as paper. I was still looking at her almost transparent whiteness when Amando said to his friend:

There's no point. My son's crazy about little Indian girls.

He went back to talking about the barge and freight prices. I remember I left the room and went with Florita into the garden. I told her I didn't want to live with Amando, either in the white palace or the house in Manaus.

Since your mother died, *seu* Amando's never loved anyone—only his damned barges.

She kissed me on the mouth, the first kiss, and asked me to be patient. Crazy about little Indian girls. I repeated those words with the taste of Florita's kiss on my lips.

With these memories, I came away from the empty house, and decided to leave work and travel to Vila Bela. I told the owner of the Cosmopolitan I was going to give up the room.

Working in the harbour was no job for a Cordovil. Your father's freighters have got a future.

I had the impression everyone knew my movements, and was surprised when the owner of the grocery store gave me a ticket to Vila Bela in the *La Plata*, along with a typed note: *Meeting at the lawyer Stelios's house at 5 in the afternoon on 24 December. AC.* Amando had everything worked out: the date of departure, the ship, the time and the meeting place. Years later I had suspicions about the authorship of the note. It might have been written by Estiliano. But the fact is I went in the expectation of talking to my father. I disembarked at Vila Bela at two in the afternoon of 24 December, and when I caught sight of the white palace, I felt the emotion and sense of oppression you feel when you return home. Here I was someone else. That is, I was myself: Arminto, the son of Amando Cordovil, grandson of Edílio Cordovil, sons of Vila Bela and the River Amazon.

I discovered my father wasn't at home when Florita, dressed only in a nightgown, gave me a tight, long embrace. I felt her strong hands moving over my back, lowered my head and whispered: Servants can sniff things out. Look what happened when we had fun that afternoon.

She loosened her grip and looked at me with a guiltless smile: Don't you want some more? Was it just that afternoon?

That afternoon produced a lifetime's jealousy. I asked if she'd known I was coming.

Neither you nor your father can live far from here, she answered.

That's what she said; then she went to get my bath ready. I noted that Amando's hammock was slung in the same place in the parlour. My room was cleaned and ready, with the mosquito net hung over the bed as if I'd never left home. In the back garden, I spoke to the caretaker and his wife. Almerindo and Talita came to live in the back of the white palace when Amando abandoned the Boa Vida plantation to dedicate himself to his freighters. Florita, out of spite or jealousy, treated the couple as if they were strangers. They hadn't lost the subservient habit of calling me 'Doctor', as they did when I was a boy. Almerindo did repairs in the house, whitewashing the façade after the winter rains. Talita looked after the garden and cleaned the stone centrepiece of the fountain. It was in the shape of my mother's head; Amando had had it made after she died. From a very young age, I used to look at the young face, the grey stone eyes which seemed to question me. I was on my knees in front of the head when I smelled the waft of scent from the Bonplant perfumery. Florita informed me that the bath was full. After the bath she served lunch: beans with pumpkin and *maxixe*, grilled fish and *farofa* with turtle eggs.

Your father's completely stuffed with food. He didn't even have a siesta.

Where is he?

In the Carmelite School. He went to see the headmistress. Then he was going to Dr Estiliano's house.

Our meeting's at five, I said, knowing Florita already knew. But I want to see the old man first.

Be careful not to turn Christmas sour, she warned me.

Is he in a good mood?

When he's in Vila Bela he's only short of hugging the moon.

I went to Ribanceira and waited in the shade of the *cuiarana* tree. Vila Bela was hiding from the hot sun. Everything was still in the afternoon heat. I remember the noise of a boat, the sounds of a river that never sleeps. The school gardener opened the gate and this tall, burly man appeared, in dark jacket and trousers. He wasn't wearing a hat. I thought this might be the moment to talk. Between us there was the shadow of my mother: the suffering he'd borne since her death. For Amando, I had put a brutal end to a love story. I was afraid of the confrontation, and hesitated. He took quick steps, his hands clenched as if the fingers had been amputated, his eyes fixed on a point somewhere in front of him. His well-combed hair looked like a helmet. My father was walking towards the white palace. As I emerged from the shade, he lifted his head towards the bell in the tower, swung round and walked towards Matadouro Street. I think he'd decided to go to Estiliano's house straight away. At the end of the square he stopped, and his crossed arms grabbed his shoulders as if he was hugging his own body. He slowly bent his legs and fell to his knees. His head was shining in the corner of the square. The man was going to collapse forwards, but he twisted and sank backwards instead. I shouted out his name and ran towards him. On his back, he lay staring at me, his face contorted in pain. I was floundering, trying to massage his chest. Then there was a single embrace, for my dead father. The man I most feared was in my arms. He was still. I hadn't the strength to carry him on my own. In a short time the town awoke and curious bystanders surrounded his body. Somebody pointlessly said that Vila Bela's only doctor had gone to Nhamundá. Florita arrived in such a state of despair that she pushed me away, screaming, and fell weeping to her knees. Estiliano appeared a few minutes later. The bystanders moved back while the big man leant over Amando, kissed his face and delicately closed his eyes.

I had spent some four or five years without setting foot in Vila Bela, and from the moment Amando's wake took place in the Carmo Church I saw how beloved he was. This left me confused, for the praises for the dead man contradicted my image of the living father. I knew he liked giving alms, a vice I inherited and kept up for a long time. And I remembered how much charity he dispensed at the festivals of Our Lady of Mount Carmel. But after his death I discovered he'd been a real philanthropist. He gave food and clothes to the Carmelite Orphanage, and contributed to the building of the bishop's palace and the restoration of the town jail. He even paid the jailers' wages, a favour he did both to the government and the locals. At the funeral, Ulisses Tupi and Joaquim Roso, river pilots Amando trusted—as well as Denísio Cão, a strange boatman from Jaguar Island—offered their condolences. Not even Amando could stand Denísio. He knelt down and crossed himself, with his long, horsy, sad face. The orphan girls from the Sacred Heart of Jesus were at the cemetery too, all wearing the same uniform: a brown skirt and a white blouse. Girls. One of them looked more grown up—like a woman with two different ages. She was wearing a white dress and was looking upwards, as if she wasn't there, as if she wasn't anywhere. Suddenly her look met mine, and the angular face smiled. I didn't know the girl. I looked at her so hard that the headmistress of the Carmo School came over to me. Mother Joana Caminal came alone, offered her condolences and said dryly: Senhor Amando Cordovil was the most generous man in this town. Let us pray for his soul.

And off she went, with the girl and the other orphans in tow.

Orphans of Eldorado

The room where he slept in the white palace was
still as he had left it. All I did was move the hammock
to another part of the room. During his siestas,
Amando's body used to obstruct the way to the
windows. I shortened the strings and brought the
hammock nearer the middle window. That way I
could see the ramp up to the Market and the river,
I could feel the life coming from the waters.

Florita reacted to her boss's death with a great
deal of sadness. She wore white clothes instead of
full mourning, and still cooked my father's favourite
dishes. Whether because she forgot, or out of habit,
sometimes she put Amando's plate and knife and
fork at the head of the table; I ate alone, not looking
at the empty place.

At the beginning of the New Year, I went with
Estiliano to Manaus. He gave me a box from the
Mandarim with the papers Amando kept in the
house. When Estiliano opened the inventory, I
discovered my father had owned a plot in the Flores
neighbourhood, near the asylum. He left a tidy sum
to his friend, along with a house on the bank of

the Francesa Lagoon. A little embarrassed, Estiliano said that the money would buy him wine for his old age. The house would be his refuge in Vila Bela.

Amando's generosity to his beloved Stelios didn't upset me. I asked the lawyer to be my representative in the firm; then I asked for money to live on, suggesting a monthly allowance. Estiliano spoke of a bank loan to pay Holtz, the shipbuilders: how could I ask for so much money? He couldn't allow it.

Get another lawyer, he said firmly. There are lots in Manaus.

But only one Stelios, I said.

We reached an agreement on how much I could take out. And he himself suggested that the money should be sent by Lloyd's internal post. I tried to insist that he should run the firm, but he refused: he wouldn't be coming to live in Vila Bela for a few years. I was the heir, I should take over . . .

I have neither the experience nor the desire, I interrupted.

Amando trusted the manager. You could live in

Vila Bela and spend a few days in Manaus. And look after the Boa Vida plantation.

I came to live here, but I couldn't go two months without a visit to Manaus. I spent them in the office, looking at the pile of papers on the desk and getting irritated with problems of all kinds: parts for machines, the dismissal or hiring of employees, missing merchandise, customs dues, taxes. The manager responded to my doubts with few words, or with a haughty silence. I was the boss before time, which confounded him. When he cornered me to make a decision, I asked Estiliano for help. The lawyer sat in my father's chair, looked at the documents I was to sign and questioned the price of transporting goods. With the voice of a croaking dog he would complain: If Amando was here ... Sometimes he criticised me because I was sharp with the manager. I couldn't divine his thoughts, and I didn't have the serenity of Estiliano to withstand the cold look that sought out my father's portrait on the office wall. Why did he look at his dead boss so often? In Vila Bela, I only thought about the manager and the firm when I saw the *Eldorado* some hundred yards from the white palace, and then I thought my life depended on that cargo-boat plying the Amazon. But I forgot the ship on the day I encountered the girl I'd seen at Amando's funeral. The woman with two ages. Dinaura. I couldn't remember her face in detail; her eyes, yes, the look in her eyes. To see again what memory has erased is a great happiness. Everything came back to me: the smile, the sharp look in the angular face, eyes more almond-shaped than mine. An Indian? I tried to find out where she was from, but never did. I found something else; something that depends merely on chance, on a single moment in life. And I saw it was too late to undo the work of destiny.

When Estiliano heard me talk of Dinaura, he was contemptuous: That's a good one, a Cordovil infatuated with a girl from the jungle. And Florita, without knowing the orphan, said that her look was just a spell: she looked like one of those madwomen who dream of living at the bottom of the river.

The look in Dinaura's eyes was what most

attracted me. Sometimes a look has the force of desire. Then desire grows and wants to penetrate the flesh of the beloved. I wanted to live with Dinaura, but I put off the decision for as long as vanity would allow me. I don't know if my life was less unhappy than hers then. It was certainly more futile. Empty. Since I'd moved here, I'd waited anxiously for the ships that came from Europe up the Amazon; when one of them berthed at Vila Bela, an officer in the port gave me the ship's menu and informed me about the passengers. His name was Arneu, a gossipy, sycophantic man, so much so you felt sorry for him. If he said he'd seen pretty girls on deck, I'd go to dine and dance in the boat's saloon. Sometimes I embarked for Manaus and had a good time at the dances in the Ideal and the Luso, went to the matinees at the Alcazar, the Rio Branco and the Polytheama, and to the operas in the Opera House. Then I'd go to the Chalet-Jardim to meet the Italian singers. One afternoon, while I was having a beer in the High Life, I saw one of the lads from the pension in the street—Juvêncio. And the worst of it was that he recognised me and came into the bar.

The young gentleman from the Saturno, he said, stretching out his hand.

I was going to shake his hand, but Juvêncio didn't want affection or courtesy, he wanted money. I gave him money and he laughed, revealing his toothless gums, and went right back to the street. Years later, I saw Juvêncio in a fight near the same bar. He was a grown man, and the High Life had gone bust.

Back at Vila Bela, I'd spend the night drinking wine and reading opera librettos, the latest *Pathé-Journal* and old newspapers. I would grow melancholy before sunrise. Then I'd go out at dawn through the dirt streets of this neglected town, as far as the Fishermen's Steps, where I saw the shapes of heads looking out of windows in the darkness—old people unable to sleep; I don't know if they were laughing or waving at me. Near the jungle, I saw the miserable shacks of the Aldeia, heard words in indigenous languages, murmurs, and when I went back to the river bank, I saw fishing boats moored by the ramp to the Market, boats laden with fruit, a steamer going down the Amazon to Belém. I had my breakfast in the Bar do Mercado, then I prowled round Sacred Heart Square, climbed up into the tree on the Ribanceira and thought about Dinaura until the sun lit the orphanage dormitory. If a Carmelite saw me sitting on a branch, I'd ask after Dinaura. The nun wouldn't answer, would look as if she'd seen the devil, and I'd say: She's going to leave the orphanage and come and live with me. Then I'd give a laugh which shocked the nun, a laugh that sounded obscene but in fact was just pure desire.

It might have been lunacy and not a caprice. I went back and forth between this idyll and my journeys to Manaus. The idyll won out. And my high life died out, along with the euphoria of an epoch. How everything changes in a short time. Some years before my father's death, people only talked of growth. Manaus, rubber exports, jobs, business, tourism, everything was growing. Even prostitution. Only Estiliano showed signs of scepticism. And he was right, that was the worst of it. In the bars and restaurants the news in the Belém and Manaus papers was repeated with alarm: If we don't plant rubber tree seeds, we'll disappear . . . So much corruption in politics, and taxes are on the increase.

At home, the words were no less bitter. One day Florita came into my room to pick up the dirty washing and said:

I've had a bad dream. Something with your enchanted woman in it.

I looked suspiciously at Florita, waiting to hear more about the dream, but she left without a word. Dreams and chance took me to a road where Dinaura always appeared. I remember having seen a woman like her at the river's edge. It was very early, a sunless morning, with thick mist. The woman walked along the bank till she disappeared in the mist. It could have been Dinaura—or my own eyes playing tricks. I remembered the *tapuia* woman who'd gone to live in the enchanted city, and ran towards the bank. But there was no one to be seen.

One Sunday afternoon Dinaura walked by the front of the white palace, smiling at me with voracious lips. She was accompanying some girls from the orphanage to the Aldeia, where the Cegos do Paraíso neighbourhood is today. I followed the group. Dinaura was reading a book in the shade of a mango tree while the girls played. She was wearing a cheap printed cotton dress, and only stopped reading to stare at the river. In the late afternoon she and the girls went down the ravine by the Fishermen's Steps. I crossed the dirt road and sat down where she'd been reading. Dinaura left her book on the sand and went into the water alone. She swam and dived for so long I began to feel out of breath. When she appeared naked, with her dress rolled up round her neck, I felt my body tremble with desire. I'm certain she saw me, because the girls were pointing at me, laughing and pinching Dinaura's bum and thighs. From afar, I licked that body in the late afternoon sun. I didn't even think about the Fishermen's Steps: I ran down the ravine, but when I got near the river, Dinaura was already dressed and walking ahead of the girls. I followed the wet dress as far as the ramp of the Ribanceira, cut down some mud steps and stopped at the top, in front of Dinaura. I said I wanted to talk to her. I saw her astonished eyes in her unearthly face, the smile on her large, moist lips; I managed to touch her shoulders before she started running to Sacred Heart Square.

In Vila Bela's port someone spread the tale that the orphan was an anaconda who was going to devour me and drag me off to a city at the bottom of the river—and that I should break the spell before I was transformed into a diabolical creature. As Dinaura spoke to no one, rumours went about that people who were silent had been bewitched by Jurupari, the god of Evil.

One Saturday, Joaquim Roso and Ulisses Tupi invited me to play dominos in Salomito Benchaya's pension. Denísio Cão, the strange boatman, pushed his way into the company and lost one game. He was a man with no luck, and went on to lose every game he played. The intruder grew irritated—he hated losing. And then, without batting an eyelid, he said:

That mother superior, the big chief, that Spanish one, is she a virgin, is she as saintly as she looks? I'll believe that when I see it . . .

The players gave the boatman a stern look; Joaquim Roso disarranged the game of dominos and left. Salomito put the pieces back in the box: they'd be better playing in the Market bar.

Denísio spat to one side and turned his face to me, laughing: Today I carried an old man and two cows to the River Ariri. The Spanish nun was there; and your orphan, too. The two of them were planting peppers in canoes filled with soil. I offered to help, but that savage Spaniard wouldn't let me. Like I said, I'll believe it when I see it . . .

Ulisses Tupi took me there. It was a parish beyond the mouth of the Espírito Santo. On a beach by the Arari, Ulisses tied the prow of the launch to the trunk of a tree. A line of old canoes rested on forked branches stuck in the sand. There was no one to be seen in the doorways of the straw-roofed shacks.

Where's that girl, and the mother superior?

Don't be in such a hurry, said Ulisses, pointing at a bird. It was a hoatzin up in the sky, white in the intense light.

I followed the heavy flight of the bird into the swampy jungle. I heard Ulisses say the bird's name and imitate its song. I lay down on the prow and shut my eyes, dizzy with the rocking of a boat. Dinaura appeared in my dream, wearing the same cotton dress. Her spellbinding eyes were a little wide, and dark, cut out of the night sky. I began to know Dinaura's face, and felt something I'd not felt in my love affairs when I was younger. I grabbed her arms and, as I pulled her towards me, I saw the image of Mother Caminal and heard a buzzing sound.

I woke up with the noise of the launch motor. I was thinking about the dream, and sweating. I got up and took a look at the beach: the canoes hanging, the shacks boarded up, the place deserted.

I think Denísio Cão's told a fib, Ulisses said.

Florita, who listened to the gossip in Vila Bela, told me that to the Carmelites I was the devil incarnate: I preyed on young girls, I was a randy bachelor with not a single drop of my father's honour in me. They said they'd seen me disembark with whores from Manaus at the ramp up to the Market, and swim with them in utter shamelessness, there on the beach of the Ponta da Piroca.

I never brought any women to Vila Bela. But perhaps a repeated lie is just an imitation of the truth? I asked Estiliano to help me convince Mother Caminal that I wasn't the devil they said I was.

The Mother Superior is responsible for the moral welfare of the orphans.

What about my feelings?

Don't be cynical, Arminto.

I insisted, feigning deference. He was a lawyer, I said, everyone listened to what he had to say.

I saw his face glow with pride. But then his brow furrowed and his eyes fixed anxiously on my face, as if reading the pages of a tragedy. He put his hands on my shoulder: he was very concerned.

I didn't know if he was talking about the firm or the orphan.

The truth is that Dinaura filled my thoughts. I

put on a white linen jacket, went to the Ribanceira and looked at the windows of the orphanage. Yes, that same building. Some idiots laughed at me. A nutcase, they said. That orphan's burnt his brains out. But when Dinaura walked through the town, men followed her round. No one spoke to the woman. Why not? Fear. Something about her inhibited anything more than a word or a gesture. They were afraid, these defeated machos. They'd meet in the Travellers' Bar in Horadour Bonplant's perfumery or in the Market Bar, lying effortlessly about their conquests. On the afternoon Dinaura met me for the first time on Sacred Heart Square, they all saw. This happened after several attempts. She would escape without saying a word. In fact, I don't know if she did escape: it was the silence that gave the impression that she had. I remember that for a long time I didn't see Dinaura in the places she usually went alone, or with the other orphan girls. Florita went to check at the school door and came back with a choked smile, full of ill-disguised malice. Only my father had ever managed to speak to Mother Caminal, she said; he was the only one the Spaniard would speak to. They understood each other.

Forget that girl. Forget her before she brings misery.

Misery? I asked.

She's not going to be your wife. Someone who belongs to nobody can never be loved.

Florita had a curious way of being jealous; and as I was always affected by everything she said, I became speechless in the presence of this woman who'd looked after me like a mother. I thought about Estiliano, and Amando's strong bond with the Mother Superior of the Carmo. The lawyer came to spend the month of July in Vila Bela, and I went to the Francesa Lagoon with some bottles of wine for him. While we sat on the veranda, drinking together in silence, I saw he was censuring me with his eyes. It was some time since I'd set foot in Manaus, and I knew that the war in Europe was damaging rubber exports—the war, and the rubber seedlings planted in Asia. It was as if he was talking about this with his eyes, this large man drinking in silence, and me divining his thoughts, his hoarse voice just about to say: It's absurd to ignore the business you've inherited from your father . . . Silently we prowled round Dinaura's name, the two of us looking at a canoe in the water, dark, smooth and calm as a sheet of copper. I drank another glass and got my courage up.

Do you know why I came here? The girl who came from the jungle. It's not a whim, Estiliano. Mother Caminal controls the orphans' lives.

He went on drinking, looking at the canoe motionless in the dark water.

Can't you give a little help to your friend's son?

He merely looked at me as an old man looks at a youth: a look that can be affable or aloof. No pain or compassion. He picked up the glass of wine, got up and went into the sitting room. I waited for some minutes, an hour, an absurd length of time, until the sky turned red. I looked towards the room: he was sitting in front of an open book, his face bent over a sheet of paper. He was copying words from the book. His bulky body filled the room, and the man went on writing, copying. When he finished, he blew onto the page to dry the ink and reread in silence, sipping his wine. He was breathing like an animal exhausted after a hunt. He came back to the veranda, handed me two sheets of paper and said in an irritated tone: Send this to the Mother Superior with a note saying your feelings are expressed in these lines.

He went back into the room and left me alone on the veranda. I read the poem right there, in the semi-darkness. A mysterious poem, copied from some Spanish book.

Florita took the poem and the note to the Carmo School. What can a poem do? For me, it performed more than a miracle. Mother Caminal asked me to come to her office to talk. The simplicity of the setting impressed me. The room looked like an improvised, poverty-stricken museum. On the floor were bits of ceramic, ritual masks and bits of the funerary urns of indigenous tribes who no longer existed. The name of the first Carmelite to preach in these parts was engraved on the wall, between oil paintings of St Teresa and St John of the Cross.

Mother Caminal offered me a seat, took up the two sheets and read out the Spanish poem in an emphatic tone. I envied the woman's voice. The images and the feeling grew with the sound of the words. She read the whole poem and, with her eyes on the paper, said:

This is Estiliano's handwriting. Your father was very fond of him; he would have liked him more, only that Greek's an agnostic.

He's not Greek, he was born in Amazonia and studied in Recife.

He was born here, but he's never prayed in our church.

Then she spoke about the orphan, an intelligent and hard-working girl. She might have been a Carmelite, a servant of the Lord. She had considered it, but had given up the idea. It's difficult to follow these girls' reasoning. One day they want one thing, the next they've forgotten it all. They pray devoutly and don't believe a thing. But, in our lives, God chooses the best way.

Where did she come from?

From some place or other.

But not on this island.

Mother Caminal returned the sheets of paper:

Read that poem from time to time, right into old age. If my orphan wants to, she can meet you at five o'clock in the square. And only on Saturdays. Never go near the orphanage dormitory, and never come in here again. You don't have to give anything to the Order. Your father gave a lot.

My story with Dinaura began that week. She wanted to date me. Now I'm just a carcass, but I was a good-looking young man then. And I was still well off. That counts for something, doesn't it? That was what I thought. But money wasn't enough. That is, it didn't go very far. We met on Saturdays; no other afternoons were allowed for our love. The orphanage regulations were severe. The bell rang to wake the girls at five in the morning. They had prayers at six, at midday and again before bedtime. After prayers, the neighbourhood would hear a nun bellowing: Praise be to Our Lord Jesus Christ, to which the choir of orphans would respond:

For ever. They ate in silence in the school refectory; when a girl wanted to go to the toilet, she slapped the table with her hand. At eight in the evening the bell rang for silence, and the head sister inspected the dormitory. I thought the orphans only prayed, sewed and studied, but they did much more than that: in the mornings they worked in the vegetable garden, dusted the altar and the statues of the saints, and helped clean the dormitory and the school-rooms. Late afternoons, after class, they went to the chapel to give thanks and pray with the Carmelites. I also learned that they had a weekly retreat. Each orphan stayed alone in a dark room, reciting a whole rosary by candlelight in front of the Heart of Jesus. It was a silent love affair. Sometimes I heard Dinaura's voice in my dreams. She had a gentle, somewhat singsong voice, which spoke of a better world at the bottom of the river. Suddenly she would grow silent, frightened by something the dream wouldn't reveal.

One Saturday she would surprise me with a smile, the next with a terrible sadness, as if she were going to die. She was prettier when she was sad, her face still, the lips in their place. She was the oldest girl in the orphanage, and the only one with permission to date. That was the way it was at the beginning: the two of us sitting on the bench in the square, holding hands, like two lovers of that time, and of this town. She never said when she'd entered the orphanage. And I grew accustomed to the silence, with the voice I only heard in my dreams.

Florita told me that several orphans spoke the *língua geral*; they studied Portuguese and were forbidden to speak in indigenous languages. They came from villages and settlements on the Andirá and Mamuru rivers, from the Ramos branch, and other places in the middle reaches of the Amazon. Only one had come from a long way off, from the Upper Rio Negro. Two of them, from Nhamundá, had been abducted by river traders and sold to businessmen in Manaus and big shots in the government. They were taken to the orphanage by order of a judge, a friend of the headmistress. In Vila Bela, Mother Caminal was known as God's Judge, because she forbade the exchange of children and women for merchandise, and reported men who beat their wives and servants. But never once did she come on a Saturday to watch us in the square.

When the bell rang at six in the afternoon, Dinaura would kneel in the direction of the church, with her eyes shut and her hands on her chest. One time, after she'd finished praying, she sat eagerly on my lap, but when I went to embrace her she jolted and ran away. I was rigid, stiff as a board. On other Saturdays, the people walking through the Sacred Heart Square would see Dinaura melt into my legs. The most sanctimonious of the women sent messages to Florita: my father was right, I took advantage of Indians and poor girls in general. To hell with that. I'd anxiously await the next Saturday, surrendering to the look from a silent face.

One day in July, a beggar from the square handed a note to Florita. It was from Dinaura. *The festival of the Patron Saint. Shall we go?* The festival was on the night of 16 July, and still lights the town every year. Pilgrims came from the interior of Amazonas and

Orphans of Eldorado

Pará. I remember my father used to bring many of
the faithful from Manaus. They ate and slept in the
boat; at night, they asked the Virgin to protect
Amando. I heard the prayers and saw the faithful
on deck with burning candles in their hands. It
looked like a boat in flames, like a great anaconda
lit up on the bank of the Amazon. In July, Amando
really had been lavish with his money. He paid for
the decoration of the square, the painting of the
Carmo Church, the monasteries and parish churches,
the new clothes for the lepers, the capes and ropes
for the devotees of the Virgin. After the Mass he
gave a huge meal of turtle meat to the people.

I was still a child when he dragged me to the
festival, twice. The second time, I ran away. He and
his servant, Almerindo, searched all round the town
for me, and only came across me in the early
morning, lying with Florita in the hammock in her
room. When he came in, I shut my eyes. Florita got
up and opened the window to quell Amando's
hatred. She said I had nausea, and an upset stomach.

Get out of that hammock, he commanded.

I obeyed, without opening my eyes. The first slap made my face burn and threw me back to the hammock; he bent over and slapped me again with the palm of his hand on the ear. The crack buzzed like an insect trapped inside my head. It was impossible to return the favour: my father was a heavy Cordovil, with thick fingers on his big hands. Then Florita confessed she'd lied. Amando threatened to throw her out of the house, and forced me to live with the servants for a month, eating their food and cleaning the yard. The first night I slept in the basement; that is, I couldn't sleep because of the heat. Every night after that I slept in a hammock out of doors. The next year, Amando made me go to the Virgin's festival again.

I remembered all this as I read Dinaura's invitation. I was a man now, and Amando Cordovil was dead.

On the afternoon of 16 July the orphans and the boarders entered the Square of the Sacred Heart of Jesus in single file. Nobody wore a uniform. I saw the daughters of the wealthy families separated from the orphans, and a circle of *tapuia* girls shrinking back, paralysed by shyness and poverty. They all loved the Patron's festival because it was the freest day in the year. They could sink their teeth into the food and the sweets; they could dance and sing till ten at night. The boldest of them ran down to the edge of the river and pushed themselves into the company of the boys from Manaus and Santarém. Three or four orphans, they say, got pregnant on the night of devotion to the Virgin, but I had no desire to know if it was true or not. What I wanted most was to see Dinaura. I heard the choir of the boarding girls; then the Tavares Trio played *modinhas* with a *cavaquinho*, a violin and a *nhapé*, an indigenous kind of maracas. As darkness fell, the bishop asked everyone to listen in silence to the penance of seven orphans.

The first recounted that one rainy night she had been possessed by the Cobra-Grande and had become so agitated that the whole island began to tremble, and as a result the river Amazon had flooded her house. She then knelt and prayed to expel this profane story from her mind. I don't remember the other penances, only the last. The lamps were already lighting the square, and by the time the girl stopped speaking my body was weak from sweating. The penitent's name was Maniva. Small and frail, she said she'd come from far away to work in a local politician's house and had ended up in the orphanage. She'd studied in the missions of the Upper Rio Negro, that's why she spoke Portuguese. Before she lived in the Vila Bela orphanage, she couldn't stop dreaming of blood. My blood was a nightmare, the penitent said. She was about twelve years old and was already an orphan when she saw blood running from her vagina and got a fright. The first blood. She felt her head throbbing, and cried out so much with the pain that her uncle took the poor girl to be cured by the village shaman. Maniva was forbidden from entering the house because menstrual blood was harmful to the shamans. It was sacred, prohibited blood. It was sent by the spirits of nature: thunder, water, fish and even the spirits of the dead. Then the shaman said that the creator of the world sucked the powder, made from crushed *paricá* leaves, from his niece's vagina when she was menstruating, asleep. Some of the powder was scattered over the lands of the peoples of the Amazon and spread throughout the forest, but only the shamans can smell the powder and see the world; only they have had the power to open people's eyes and then transform, create and cure other beings. The girl heard this: when the shaman sucks the blood, the dust, he dies; that is to say, his soul leaves his body and travels to the other world, older than this one, the beginning of everything. He opens his arms to the clouds, embraces the sky and sings; he sits and smells several times the powder with the bone from a falcon's leg, and so brings the other world into this one. Looking at the moving clouds, the shaman said he was in a sacred, eternal world, and so could act in the human world. He saw what I couldn't see, what none of us can see, said Maniva. He saw the bones in his own body, and saw his soul journeying to a far distant place, until it reached the mouth of the river that flows in the depths of the earth.

Then he went on climbing up a ladder, on the way to the other heaven. The most ancient shaman lives up there, on the final ladder. A sky all white and silvery. A new world. A world without disease.

When the shaman stopped speaking, Maniva's head was no longer throbbing. She never felt pain again. But the bloody nightmares tormented her life. After her uncle died, she went to Manaus, and then came to Vila Bela with a river trader. She journeyed on, dreaming of blood until she found Mother Caminal and prayed with her to erase the nightmare. She didn't want to remember the shaman's words. She crossed herself, knelt down and wept, her body shaking; then she stretched her arms skyward and shouted out the name of God and the Virgin of Mount Carmel. The pilgrims' and orphans' applause was accompanied by shouting, and I thought about the penitent and bloody nightmares. Maniva, the pilgrims, the orphans, the nuns—was everyone going mad? It was like a hallucination as, amidst the acclamation of the Virgin, the scent of lavender sent a shiver down my spine, and I turned round to find Dinaura's lips touching my face. She appeared without my noticing, and caressed me with warm hands that made me feverish. I felt Dinaura's body and began to sweat, and she only went away when three drummers and a dancer entered the bandstand. They were musicians from the *quilombo* Silêncio do Matá, and they were the surprise of the night. One of the men lit a torch and used its heat to stretch the snakeskin of the drums. The dancer announced that they were going to perform a homage to the Virgin. Then she began to dance, alone, in the middle of the bandstand, for some minutes. The musicians remained silent. Then, in unison, the sound of the drums burst out, loud as thunder. Dinaura gripped my arm with her sweaty hand; her thigh was trembling, her feet were tapping the ground. Suddenly, she let go of me, ran to the bandstand and began to dance. The shouting that burst out had nothing to do with religious devotion. She imitated the movements and rhythm of the other woman, her shoulders bared; she wasn't looking at me, but at the sky. I don't think she saw a thing, nobody at all. She was blind to the world, possessed by the dance. They danced together as if they had it rehearsed. At the end they embraced, and Dinaura left, behind the bandstand. She disappeared. How was I to understand such a changeable woman, with such an unstable soul? I went to talk to the musicians and the dancer, but they didn't know Dinaura. The orphans and the boarders went into the school, the pilgrims went back to the boats or to their homes. I stayed alone in the square . . . You want to understand someone, but all you find is silence.

I still remember the afternoons of longing and desolation, the slowly passing days and the nights of broken sleep. The four or five telegrams sent from Manaus, which I tore up in a rage without reading, without even opening them. Florita's nervous voice asking: What if it's something urgent?, saying: I bet Dr Estiliano wants to speak to you, and her searching for the bits of paper, trying to put words together, to decipher their meaning. One afternoon in December, I got to the square earlier, lay down on the warm seat and went to sleep. As I was awoken by the clock striking five, Dinaura's face appeared against the sun. I had no time to ask about the dance, or to get up; I saw her black eyes, large and frightened. Could it be a dream? But I didn't want a dream, I wanted her there, clear as day. Then I stroked Dinaura's mouth with my fingers, felt her anxious breathing, the tremor and the sweat on the open lips as they brushed against my face. In the pleasure of the kiss, I felt a ferocious bite. I let out a cry, more out of fright than pain. I tried to speak; my tongue was bleeding. In the confusion, Dinaura escaped.

In the Carmo College, one of the boarding girls claimed I'd forced Dinaura to kiss me. One Friday morning, Florita heard that she wanted to journey to the submerged city.

Who told you that crazy story?

Iro. The messenger that lives in the square.

I went after Iro, but Estiliano caught me on the ramp going up to the Market and took me to the quay. He was on board the steamship *Atahualpa* and

was going to spend some days in Belém before moving
to Vila Bela. He asked if I'd not read the telegrams,
adding: The manager wants to speak to you. He can't
pay the employees any longer, or send your money.

Is the firm in trouble?

Rubber exports have plummeted.

I was suspicious: Estiliano hadn't told me everything. I was more anxious than he was, and struggled
to swallow my curiosity.

Tomorrow the *Anselm* will berth in Vila Bela and
then go on up to Manaus, he said.

I looked at Estiliano in annoyance: Tomorrow?
Saturday? I can't.

That girl's intoxicated you, Arminto.

Again I heard his hoarse voice, insisting that I
should go. Estiliano was right: I was drunk on
Dinaura; I wanted to know why she hid her past,
why the dance, the kiss, the ferocious bite that drew
blood from my tongue. I didn't have dinner with
Florita or try to get her to talk. Saturday dawned
cloudy, and the *Anselm*, in the harbour, was taking
wood on board for fuel. Arneu came by the white

palace to ask if I wanted to take lunch on board ship. I told him I was going to eat at home. Were any passengers going to stay in town?

Arneu pointed to three passengers: an old man, a woman and a lad.

The Becassis, a family from Belém, he said. The woman's name is Estrela, the son is Azário. It's said they're going to live in Vila Bela.

For the first time I saw, in the distance, Estrela's curly hair; she was hand in hand with her son. The older Becassis was behind the cart carrying the luggage. The vision of Estrela made me forget my deranged state. Arneu was staring stupidly at the stranger's body; he began saying that she was the prettiest woman on the *Anselm*, and that she'd send the men of Vila Bela mad. I didn't like hearing that. He had his uses, but he had a mania for making up to any woman he met. And he liked to show off, drooling over women who weren't for him. How big a tip had he got just for giving information about passengers? As he moved away, I followed the three foreigners with my eyes. On the pavement in front of the Travellers' Bar, the old man stopped to talk with Genesino Adel. Then he went with his daughter and grandson to Salomito's pension.

I lunched with no appetite, and as it was too early to go to the square, I lay down in the hammock in the parlour and thought about Estrela; I was thinking about her so as not to suffer more disappointment at the hands of Dinaura. The wind from the river increased the heat in the room. Was it obstinacy on my part that I wasn't on board the *Anselm*? Passion and desire were more likely reasons. The whistle, the roar of the engines, the sound, like a waterfall, of the wheels at the sides, everything was gradually blotted out. The smoke from the chimney covered the open window, and I felt my body dulled as a heavy sleepiness took me to a strange place. I could clearly see Estrela's hair waving in the water like flames. As I looked at the face, I recognised Dinaura, and heard her voice saying calmly that we could only live in peace in a city at the bottom of the river. Afterwards, in the swirling, muddy waters, I saw the stern face of a man with a threatening look.

I uttered something out loud, gasped for air, and the image disappeared. I was alone in an unknown town. I woke up with my mouth open, breathing like an asthmatic. I felt my wet shirt and saw Florita's face.

I heard the shouts of someone drowning and came to help you.

Speaking that way, she seemed to divine my dreams. I was frightened by Florita's words—the fear of someone who knows us too well. To put her off the scent, I asked her to perfume the bathwater with cinnamon essence. When she saw me all dapper and perfumed, she said I shouldn't leave the house.

Why?

She didn't answer. And I trusted to my intuition. Before five o'clock, I went to the Ribanceira and leant against the trunk of the *cuiarana* tree, in the spot where I'd seen Amando die. On the ground were flowers torn down by the wind. A sky just like this afternoon: big, thick clouds. Matadouro Street was deserted. I was so anxious that I shook when I heard the stroke of five. Then she appeared alone, in a white dress, her arms bare. We sat down under the tree; its trunk was covered in flowers. I caressed Dinaura's arms and shoulders, and wondered at her face. The desire in her eyes grew. I asked nothing, said nothing. Any word was inadequate to my urgent love. There was a strong wind blowing. She wasn't frightened by the thunder, nor did she avoid my embrace. I kept the words in my thoughts. One day we would travel together, we'd get to know other cities. She was looking at the other side of the Amazon, as if in a dream. We were going to get married and then live in Manaus or Belém, or in Rio, who knows? The rain approached, making a noise like a waterfall. It seemed we were alone in the town and the world. She lay down on the wet earth, the cloth of her dress clinging to her dark skin; she took her clothes off unhurriedly, her petti-coat, corset and bra, and stood up, naked, and took off my clothes and licked and sucked me with intense desire; then we rolled on the ground to the low wall of the Ribanceira, and then back to the tree, making love as if we were starved for it. I don't know how

long we were there, entwined, feeling the warmth
of the inner flesh. I hardly noticed the beauty of
her body, so stunned was I by the way she made
love. A dancer. Jealousy burned me up. I wanted to
forget all that and looked at the sky, the tree, the
church tower. The wet flowers fell down and covered
my eyes. I awoke with the cracking sound of the
rain on my face, and unwisely kissed Dinaura with
an almost violent desire. I wanted to touch her skin,
kiss her body. I wanted more. Her eyes said no. I
put my ear close to Dinaura's lips, but the rain deaf-
ened us. So did what I could read on her lips—a
story. What about? She got dressed and made a
gesture: I was to wait for her, she'd come back soon.
She ran off, as if fleeing from something threatening. I went after her and stopped in the middle
of the square. I returned, got dressed and waited
for her in the same spot. It was still raining when
someone appeared in the entrance to the school. I
called for Dinaura, came closer, and saw a man
who'd fallen down. He was kneeling. The beggar-
cum-messenger was gripping a smashed black

umbrella. Iro let out some groans; he was waiting for some leftover food from the school refectory. I took a damp banknote from my pocket and threw it into his belly.

God is the Father.

A strange character. He got up, crossed the square, stopped in the Rua do Matadouro and let out a laugh, with no meaning or object to it. I stood in front of the Carmo School, wondering what Dinaura's secret could be. Or the story she wanted to tell. I felt no guilt: I felt jealous of someone I might know, but I didn't know who it was. I remembered every face I knew, I hated all the men in Vila Bela, I brooded over my anger and jealousy. As I was going back home, I saw two men drinking from bottles. I went into the Travellers' Bar, asked for a bottle of wine and unhurriedly drank it, sitting on the pavement, defying the looks of Adel and his customers. They were looking at me, laughing, and I could hear mockery in their laughter. What were they laughing at? Old Genesino, the owner of the bar, provoked me:

Everyone's talking about your marriage to the orphan.

Who's talking? Your shitty customers?

He stroked his moustache and banged on the cash register:

People like your grandfather'd better keep away from here.

I left the bottle on the pavement and went into the bar. Genesino Adel came round to the front of the bar to face me, but one of his sons separated us.

Edílio Cordovil's bad reputation was still alive in the memory of the older people. I left, still stunned with other memories: the wet skin, the scent of lavender, the body kissed and possessed so eagerly in the rainy night. I went home and slumped into the hammock in the parlour. I awoke on a Sunday of deluging rain. It rained all day and night for a whole week. The Amazon dragged everything away: remains of houses on stilts, canoes and drifting boats, rafts with cattle tied to them, bellowing in terror. Santa Clara Harbour was submerged, and the rivers Macurany and Parananema flooded the lower part of the town. The caretakers tied hammocks under the eaves and spent the night singing and praying for the rain to stop. And when it stopped, Florita and I went to the top of the ravine. The Carmelites' school and the orphanage, near the bank, weren't flooded. But along the edge of the rivers, Vila Bela was an amphibious town. The slaughter-house was a sea of mud with carcasses and bits of flesh under a sky full of vultures. Limbs and entrails were floating in the dirty water, right up to the doorway of the mayor's house. The rotting remains were buried far from the town, but the mayor still had to leave his house because of the stink. I remember the episode because at that time I tried to speak to Dinaura and, while I was waiting for news, I had to put up with the foul stench coming from the slaughterhouse. Then I found out that she was going into complete reclusion—a month without seeing anyone. It wasn't an order from the headmistress, it was Dinaura's own decision. But the worst news came in a telegram from the manager of the firm: *Shipwreck* Eldorado *in Pará. Come urgently to Manaus.*

The rumours in the port contradicted one another. Some said that the captain of the *Eldorado* had been drunk; that he'd gone out of his way to see a lover at São Francisco da Jararaca; that the rain and the excessive cargo had caused the accident. A captain from the Ligure Brasiliana fleet gave me more precise information: the *Eldorado* had crashed into a sandbank at the end of Caim Island, between Curralinho and Farol do Camaleão, near Breves, in the lower reaches of the Amazon. The cargo and the ship were lost. I heard that, in the Travellers' Bar, Genesino Adel's family had celebrated the loss.

They celebrated your misfortune, said Florita. What are you waiting for? Get a boat to Manaus straight away.

My indecision lasted a few days; Estiliano was in Belém and I didn't know when he was coming back. Early one morning, Florita saw me in the hammock in the parlour and sat on the floor of the room. Before dawn arrived, she said in a calm voice that

I should embark for Manaus on the next boat. She said the same thing so many times over that I convinced myself she was right. Money. That's what it was. I didn't want to leave . . . The night of love with Dinaura, the desire to be with her, and the other nights of our life . . . But how could I live without money?

Florita got me out of the hole. She said she was going to get the house ready for the wedding to Dinaura: a month's absence couldn't drown a love of that sort. I embarked on the *Índio do Brasil* with these words in my head, and in the sleepless night I spent as I went up river, I read a novel Estiliano had lent me. I remember the words of one of the characters, a father: *I don't want you to remain here, a useless, unhappy, lacklustre son. You have to continue our name and make the business prosper.* Reading this made me downhearted, worried. And that was how I got to Manaus one late afternoon. I sent a boy to tell the firm manager that I was coming to the office the next morning. But that day I was jinxed. I was more than an hour late because of a disturbance in the centre.

Orphans of Eldorado

A group of agitated people were running around and shouting on Seventh of September Avenue. I thought it was a protest, or a parade. It was in fact the lynching of a thief. I saw the fellow almost naked, tied to a cart and being pulled along by a horse. They were stoning the poor man and whipping him with his belt. The animal was whinnying, but it didn't drown out the human suffering. Afterwards the police dragged the thief, the horse and the cart away. As they passed by me, I recognised the lad from the Saturno pension. Juvêncio couldn't even see who I was: his red eyes, in his swollen head, looked dead already.

The manager watched the scene from his office window. For the first time he faced me, his face tense, and his hands in his trouser pockets. He didn't even sit down as he told me that the Lloyd Brasileiro, the Amazon Navigation Company and other large businesses had lowered their freight charges. My father hadn't renewed the insurance on the *Eldorado*, and the firm still owed a lot of money to the English bank.

Did Estiliano not know about this?

It was Dr Cordovil's business. Your father wouldn't allow any one to sign insurance documents. He was going to renew it, but he died before he could.

The manager went on: when the *Eldorado* went under, Adler's lost eighty tons of rubber and Brazil nuts, and had started a lawsuit against the company; the port duties hadn't been paid to the Manaus Harbour . . . This litany of disasters irritated me. I knew of nothing; ignorance was my weakness. The manager stopped speaking, sat down and rested his elbows on the desk and his fingers on his forehead, casting a longing look of admiration at my father's photograph. I couldn't face Amando, even on the wall. I murmured: The firm's finished. I heard someone say in a low voice: Coward.

I asked the manager what he'd just said.

He remained silent, in the same position. The portrait of my father seemed to challenge me. Coward. You're no good for anything. It was the voice of Amando Cordovil. The same words. Or was my memory repeating what I'd so often heard?

So, that morning, I went with the manager to the English bank.

The loan. Just thinking about it puts me in a state. I think it's going to rain. This heat, the humidity . . . When it gets hot like this, I have to have a drink, if not I can hardly breathe. I used only to drink wine. Now I have a few sips of *tarubá*, good stuff I get from the *sateré-maué* Indians. It relieves the wheezing. And memories come without bringing despair with them. Then I quieten down and shut my eyes. I can talk with my eyes shut.

I felt the same breathlessness when the bank manager showed me the documents Amando had signed. The debt amounted to a fortune. I left in a daze, took a tram to the house and waited for Estiliano in Manaus.

Some ten days later he appeared. He already knew everything: I'd been naive or irresponsible. I'd been both, I thought. But I made sure I pointed out that only my father renewed the insurance.

I came earlier because I read the news about the

shipwreck in the Belém papers, he said. Then he revealed he'd been in Manaus for a week.

I didn't want to waste time, he went on. I've spoken to the judge, the bank directors and Adler's.

He explained that the two barges were moored in the Manaus Harbour, confiscated by the law. Those old barges weren't worth much, but it was possible to sell them. What was really worth something was the German freighter: the *Eldorado*.

I accused the manager of carelessness; he could have avoided those debts. Estiliano didn't get worked up: the manager was my father's shadow, and a shadow can't think about everything.

But did we have to sell the two barges?

You're going to have to sell everything: this house, the firm's offices and the land in Flores.

How could I allow that? I wanted to marry Dinaura, go travelling with her.

You're living in another world, said Estiliano. If you don't sell everything, you could be arrested. The small river transport firms in the Amazon have all gone bust. Get out of this house and take a walk round the city. That girl's removed your brain; she's deprived you of your reason. You're blind.

Estiliano was obsessed by my father's story, but he knew that even Amando couldn't have avoided bankruptcy. It wasn't fate—there's no fate in this story. Amando's dream and the lineage of the Cordovils were of no interest. My problem now was lack of money.

I went round the city by tram, saw the houses on stilts and the shacks in the suburbs and along the creeks in the centre, and camps where ex-rubber-tappers slept; I saw children being shooed off as they tried to beg for food or money in front of the Alegre Bar, the Italian Food Manufactory. The prison on Seventh of September Street was full, and several houses and shops were for sale. All this only increased the longing I felt for Dinaura. I sent her a letter, telling her what had happened; I wrote that I was dying to see her, that I loved her very much, more than I could say, much more than I even knew. And that I couldn't come back to Vila Bela just yet.

I was defeated by the wait. I left the house to go

with Estiliano to the tribunal, and avoided going by the firm's offices. The last time I'd been there I'd insulted the manager, and wanted to sack him from the place and job which, in reality, had never belonged to me.

Estiliano pulled me over to a corner of the room and whispered:

In a disaster it's best to act with your head.

I envied that man his cool-headedness, the logic some god had given him. I never saw the manager again. They say he died at the end of the First World War, of the Spanish flu.

A month later, Estiliano made an agreement with Adler's and the English bank. I was lucky, he told me, they hadn't questioned the valuation of the property.

I haven't even enough money to go back to Vila Bela.

Let's auction off what's in the house and the office furniture.

He'd already bought my return ticket. I could get some money for the piano and the porcelain in the house. And there were my mother's rings.

It's a lot for someone who's done nothing, he added, with calm brutality. And there's still the house in Vila Bela. A valuable property.

And the Boa Vida plantation, I said angrily.

An Italian businessman picked up the objects that were auctioned; for the first time since my father's death, I counted the money note by note, fearfully doing calculations. Back at Vila Bela, Florita greeted me unenthusiastically. The façade of the white palace hadn't been whitewashed; the walls in the parlour and the bedrooms were stained with damp.

You never sent any money for the upkeep of the house, she said.

That's not why you've got that face on you.

She stopped, searching for words, and I didn't feel like waiting.

What's happened?

Seeing how edgy I was, she backed up to the wall. Once Florita chose to dig her heels in, she would do everything short of swallowing her own tongue. I could read nothing in her eyes. I ran to the Carmelite School, crossed the patio and ran up the stairs of the orphans' building. The girls were sitting in a circle. They were sewing in silence. When they saw me, they got up and hid in the hammock. Only one of them stood up, stiffly, her hands gripping the scapular of the Virgin of Mount Carmel. We looked at each other as if we were crazy. I asked after Dinaura.

She doesn't live here. She never slept . . .

Never slept?

I heard whispering, muttering. Suddenly, they all went quiet. The woman gradually appeared, slowly ascending the stairs: her green, observant eyes in her dark face, the silver crucifix, her thin body covered by a brown habit. Her body was almost as tall as mine. She walked alongside Mother Caminal, the ruling sister. She was the sister who had asked me to leave the dormitory. I wanted no trouble or scandal. In the doorway, Mother Caminal gave me the news:

Dinaura's out there somewhere.

In Vila Bela?

No one knows.

I looked at the nun and asked her in a very loud voice why she was lying to me.

You didn't deserve that girl. How can you be the son of Amando Cordovil?

My father's name threw me into confusion. His name, and the question accompanying it. The church bell seemed a shadow hidden in the yellow tower. Iro, the beggar who'd been there on that rainy night, was sitting on a bench in the square, his useless umbrella stuck under his arm. He stretched out his bony hand; I carried on walking as he threw the umbrella towards me shouting: You're going to die of drowning.

I turned to face him.

Drowning, you tight-fisted son of a bitch.

I kicked the umbrella, and on the Ribanceira I stopped under the *cuiarana* tree and pondered Dinaura's destiny. I avoided looking at the bench in the square, not wanting to remember Iro's words. But something tempted me. I went to look for him, but the bench was empty. The fear overtook the longing I felt for Dinaura. The fear of not finding her, the fear of the beggar's words.

At home, Florita told me I had the face of a

suffering soul. Did she know that Dinaura had fled? That she no longer slept in the orphanage? She wouldn't answer; she just gave me the envelope with the letter I'd sent to Dinaura. Still sealed. Iro left it here, Florita said. An unread love-letter is a bad omen.

Then I told her what the beggar had said to me.

Die of drowning? We're going to live in misery, that's the truth of it.

I was still the owner of the plantation and the white palace. It wasn't just a whim, wanting to keep the house. The white palace was where I'd spent my childhood, but I couldn't look after the property. Almerindo and Talita planted manioc and bananas, kept pigs and chickens. That was their food; they exchanged any that was left over for fish. But I gave them rice, beans, sugar, coffee and soap. They hardly spoke to me; they came in and out of the back of the house as if they owned the garden. For them, I was a despised weakling of a son, lacking the heavy hand of the Cordovils. Almerindo let his relatives from the interior into the garden. They sang and talked in loud voices, making an insolent racket. My father, I remember, used to put up with the noise. Sometimes, he gave a guitar to the caretaker and a pair of shoes to Talita; before the elections he went to the garden to ask for votes for one of the candidates. This intimacy irritated me, because it was born of self-interest, calculated. At bottom, they were only servants. I asked Florita when I should put the couple out in the street.

Today, this minute. Talita hates me because she thinks I'm your lover. And he hates me because I caught him stealing your old clothes.

Why did you let him?

Because Amando let Almerindo get his hands on his worn shirts. Your father used to say: He thinks he's robbing them, I think I'm giving them away.

So I told the caretakers to go and live at the plantation. But they refused; they'd only budge if I found a house and jobs for them. The solution was to talk to Leontino Byron, the politician Amando had favoured. Byron dreamed of great things. A deputy, that was what he wanted to be. I asked him to help

my late father's caretakers. The politico greeted me
with effusive embraces. He said these words: My
friend, who doesn't owe favours to Amando? Then
he got them a little wooden house at the edge of
town. And some hard work: cleaning the cemetery.
At the back of the house they had food and a basement; in the cemetery, a miserable salary. Not much
of a choice, but I did get rid of the couple who
worshipped Amando.

I began to look around town for Dinaura. I went
from door to door, where people still remembered
Amando's presents and favours: a job in the civil
service, a wedding dress, a toy, a hammock, a ticket
for the boat, even money. I was looking for my lover,
and all I heard was Amando's name. Florita swore
she wasn't in Vila Bela.

How do you know?

When you dream of another world, you can't stay
here. Much less if you're a lover having second
thoughts.

She waited for my questioning look and added:
Dinaura's gone to live in the enchanted city.

Florita wasn't being serious, but she did manage to convince me that Dinaura wasn't in Vila Bela. Then I called Joaquim Roso and Ulisses Tupi. And, against my will, Denísio Cão. These pilots knew out-of-the-way places, backwaters and little creeks, and having lived so long with the Indians and river dwellers, understood the *língua geral*. When Florita saw the three boats in the middle of the Amazon, she said: All this for a woman who's left you?

Florita's jealousy wasn't as strange as Estiliano's silence, which was terrible. In my mind, he didn't like Dinaura. Was it just the spite of an old bachelor? Or anger at the woman who'd kept me away from the business and from Manaus?

I anxiously awaited news of the boatmen. The first to appear was Denísio Cão. I found him leaning on the boat-rail, smoking. Where was she?

With his lips, Denísio gestured to a hammock on deck. I approached, peered in and saw the frightened face of a girl. He didn't wait for my question, put out his cigarette and said the little Indian was just like my girlfriend. And she was a virgin, nobody had interfered with her, not even the river dolphins. She was a girl from the Caldeirão branch of the river, a village below the Parintins hills.

She lost her mother, said the boatman. Her father offered her to me.

I felt my blood rising—the bad blood of the Cordovils. I knew that Denísio didn't carry a knife in his belt. I slapped the liar's face.

How much did you pay for this poor creature?

He confessed: he'd given some odd change to the girl's father, and on the way to Vila Bela he'd abused the unfortunate girl. Almost a child, her eyes were shut with fear and shame. I took her to the white palace and went to tell the police. But walking into the public jail, I gave up any idea of justice. The building was a pigsty; and the jailers, poor devils— they looked more like prisoners than the prisoners themselves. I contracted an old pilot I trusted and sent the girl back to the Caldeirão. The worst of it was that Denísio jumped off his boat and went round town laughing about it, full of himself, the author of so much cruelty.

Orphans of Eldorado

Joaquim Roso came back some days later with another nightmare: a nameless girl from a village on the Uaicurapá, the river where the Boa Vida plantation is. The girl made me dizzy: a sad angel with a dark little face, full of pain and silence. She'd lost her mother and been deflowered by her father. When Joaquim Roso found out, he decided to free the girl from her animal of a father.

I didn't find Dinaura, but I did perform this act of charity, he said.

It disturbed me: this was the destiny of so many impoverished daughters in Amazonia. I asked myself why a father could feel this strange desire to possess his own child. It could only be evil thoughts, a rage sent by the devil himself. I sent Florita to the Carmelite School: she was to ask Mother Caminal to look after the girl. Then I waited for Ulisses Tupi, famous for being able to navigate the labyrinth of our rivers. He appeared unexpectedly, his beard so bushy that it hid his eyes. He looked like a different person. He swore that Dinaura was alive, but not in our world. She was living in the enchanted city and was treated like a queen, but she was an unhappy woman. He heard this in the riverside houses, in the most distant settlements; he heard it from solitary *caboclos* who live with their shadows and visions. Dinaura has been seduced by an enchanted being, they said. She was the prisoner of one of those terrible animals that lure women to the bottom of the river. And they described the place where she lived: a city with so much gold and light it gleamed, and with pretty streets and squares. The Enchanted City was a legendary place, the same one I'd heard about in my childhood. It rose up in almost everyone's mind, as if happiness and justice themselves were hidden in this charmed place. Ulisses Tupi wanted me to talk to a shaman: his spirit could go to the bottom of the river to break the spell and bring Dinaura back to our world. He suggested I went to look for Dom Antelmo, the great shaman and medicine man from Maués. He knew the secrets of the bottom of the river and could talk to Uiara, the chief of all the enchanted people living in the submerged city.

When this news spread through Vila Bela, I was persecuted by a mass of rumours. Some said Dinaura had abandoned me for a toad, a big fish, a dolphin or an anaconda; others whispered that she appeared at midnight in an illuminated boat and told the fishermen she couldn't bear living in solitude at the bottom of the river. I remember the morning that Florita found a basket full of fish at the door of the white palace. Fish with their guts spilled, gills and bloody entrails, the smell of burst roes, pure gall. What the devil was this?

Your beloved sent it you, said Florita. She's tired of being half-woman half-animal.

Was Florita provoking me? The belief in super-natural beings disappeared in the morning and returned at night. We threw the fish to the vultures at the slaughterhouse. After the smell of guts and gall had disappeared, I received letters and messages from people who'd been seduced and then pursued by beings from the bottom of the river. One preg-nant woman, afraid of giving birth to a baby with a dolphin's face, wrote that she slept at the edge of the Amazon and sang to the river as the sun rose. A man who dreamed of an ancient inscription on a stone in the River Nhamundá who said he was immortal because enchanted people don't die. One guy who thought he was Casanova, who became impotent when a woman in white appeared during the night. And several stories of men and women, all of them victims of an enchanted being who appeared in dreams, singing the same love song. They were attracted by the voice and the smell of seduction, and some went mad with these visions and asked for help from a shaman.

I spent money on the boatmen. And what did they bring back for me? Myths and raped girls. Florita asked me to stop this madness and give up once and for all: Dinaura would never come back.

I didn't give up. And even afterwards, when time had drowned the yearning and the hope, and my body asked for some rest, my heart didn't dry up. My thoughts ran after her, after my desire for her. I went on Saturdays to Sacred Heart Square with the hope of seeing her in the late afternoon. I lived for some time with this crazed illusion, and avoided the beggar sitting on the same bench, the umbrella in tatters in his lap.

When I had no money left, I realised that a good deal of time had passed. I made a proposal to Estiliano: we could start up the Boa Vida plantation again, and export meat.

What are we going to use for money? For the pasture, the animals, transporting the cattle when the river's high, the employees?

And what am I going to live off?

You could sell one of the properties. Even Horadour Bonplant wants to sell his perfumery. In this place, only politicians can afford to go to sleep and wake in a good mood.

Estiliano looked at me pessimistically, which was more painful than an outright insult. Was he foreseeing my future? He noticed that the pallor in my face was caused by some terrible remembrance which, unintentionally, he was excavating in my memory.

You should visit the plantation, he said. Then you can decide if it's better to sell it.

He gave me money to hire a boat, pay a pilot and buy food. I took Florita and the box from the Mandarim shop, with documents I'd not read. Amando's papers.

The plantation was in the flood plain of the Uaicurapá. One night long ago, I can't remember when, I saw Amando pointing at the sky and comparing the size of Boa Vida to the moon. The difference is that there's a lot of water and fish here, and I'm going to harvest a lot of cocoa, he said. Florita thought he was going mad, addressing the moon and talking about planting cocoa. Pests destroyed this agricultural dream. Only the house survived, with the veranda and the parlour facing the river.

It was such a long time since I'd set foot in Boa Vida. Florita looked at the old pastures with sadness: nothing but wild grass and the burnt stumps of trees. The cocoa trees, their leaves rusted, were dead. The termites had overrun the walls and beams of the house. While Florita and the pilot were cleaning the rooms and the veranda, I looked at the old silk-cotton tree beside the river.

It's the highest tree in the world, my father used to say. Some scumbag who worked in Boa Vida messed with your mother. He was hanged from a high branch. He was already dead when I put a bullet through the rope. The body fell into the water and was later put on a raft that the river took away with it. Two men followed the raft and had some fun aiming at the corpse's neck. Way down the river, near the Paraná branch of the river, they stuck the scoundrel's head on a stake. The vultures had a good time, and no one ever messed with your mother again. No one. She lived for me until the day she gave birth to you.

Amando's rifle, hat and boots were hanging on the wall. And his portrait hung there too, between the weapon and the hat. Did Estiliano know that story? And Florita and Mother Caminal? What does one friend know about another? Or did he keep silent? I didn't feel right in Boa Vida. A beautiful place, with scarlet ibis and *jaçanãs* in the sky and the trees. The dark, shimmering waters of the Uaicurapá, the island which appeared when the river was low, when I speared fish with a harpoon and played alone on the beach. Wild Muscovy duck and teal screamed in the high branches of the silk-cotton tree. The tree must still be there, shading the house that some tenant farmers had occupied since the Second World War. It wasn't the place itself that upset me: it was my memories of it. The employees' children came up to the veranda and stopped and stared at the house. Silent children, offspring of silent men. The only real voice was Amando's—the voice that was to be obeyed. They say the cocoa plantation failed in a very short time. Then my father burnt the forest to make pasture. He was successful, even buying a barge to transport rubber, Brazil nuts and wood from the middle reaches of the Amazon to Belém. The Boa Vida became a country retreat. The hanged man— decapitated. Amando liked recounting this episode over and over again, and one time he addressed himself neither to the moon nor to me: he was speaking to my mother, as if she were still alive. I believed that story, and I remembered another:

the one about the severed head. Different stories, but Amando's words frightened me even more. Because he believed in what he was saying. And because he was oblivious to my fear.

That night, I tried to sleep in my parents' bedroom; in the morning I was woken by a sound of hissing. A bat, twisting in flight, had got caught in the wire netting over the window and let out a squeal. Its fiery eyes flashed. I lit a lamp, and the figure of an armed man appeared on the wall. It wasn't the river pilot. It was no one. Just my father's rifle and hat. Shadows. The bat disappeared. I threw the rifle and the hat onto the ground, I wanted no shadows in the room. Outside, by the edge of the river, a woman passed by. I jumped out of the hammock, my heart in my mouth, and went up to the wire netting. The woman walked towards the window. I was about to shout Dinaura's name.

I heard a little noise, said Florita.

It was just a dream. Go back to sleep.

I hung the hammock on the veranda and lay down. Memories of the Boa Vida kept me awake, with my eyes open: the noise of the cicadas and the toads, the smell of the fruit I pulled off the trees, the crack of the Brazil nuts falling out of the hands of monkeys. Before it grew light, I listened to the cries of the Muscovy ducks and watched the outline of the silk-cotton tree grow in the reddening sky, the sun still hidden beneath the horizon. The afternoon Amando plunged into the forest to bring back some employees who had fled. He came back with empty hands. Nearly empty: an ill-dressed barefoot girl came with him. She'd been captured by Almerindo, the one who later became caretaker in Vila Bela. Poor and courageous, she is, said Amando. She didn't want to flee with that lazy lot, left her family to come and work and have a better life.

My father took the girl to the white palace and bought her clothes and sandals. In Vila Bela she studied and got a name, with a Christian baptism and a party to celebrate. Amando said she was a trustworthy little girl, and he respected and even rewarded such trustworthiness. This girl brought me

up; she was the first woman I had a memory of—
Florita. One afternoon in Vila Bela, years later, when
she was asleep in the hammock, I went into the
room and stood looking at her naked body. I was
shocked when she got up, removed my clothes and
took me into the hammock. Almerindo and Talita
heard and told my father everything. Florita didn't
apologise, nor did the boss punish her. Months later,
Amando forced me to go and live in the Pension
Saturno, in Manaus.

These memories woke me early. And, since I
couldn't get to sleep, I searched through the documents kept in the Mandarim box. I read letters sent
by church dignitaries, charity houses and the Vicar-
General of the Middle Amazon. They were thanking
Amando for his donations. I found messages from
customs officers, mayors, deputies. And, at the
bottom of the box, a letter signed by a top civil
servant, and another by the governor of the state
of Amazonas. They mentioned competition for the
transport of goods to England, and that 'everything
should be planned in secret'. I was thinking about

this when I heard Florita ask what day we were to
go back to Vila Bela.

Today, I said.

I dug two holes between the silk-cotton tree and
the river, and in one of them I buried the boxes
with the pile of papers; in the other, the hat, the
rifle and the boots. I was going to bury Amando's
photograph too, with his face down, next to the
earth. But Florita wanted to keep it.

Why, if you don't visit his grave any more?

Vila Bela Cemetery's just an overgrown wilder-
ness, she said.

She lied, looking at Amando's image. She went
to the cemetery and left bromelias on her boss's
grave. She even planted a cashew-tree beside the
tomb of the Cordovils. One morning when I went
to visit my mother's grave, Florita was there, on her
knees, praying and watering the tree. I hadn't
forgotten what she told me straight after Amando's
funeral: Your father was greedy as a tapir, but I
learned to like him.

She learned to like him, in spite of his meanness.

The whole of Amazonia learned too. I gave the photograph to Florita and looked at Boa Vida as you look at a place that shouldn't be remembered any more. On the journey back to Vila Bela, I thought about the mother I'd never known. I wondered if she'd died to get away from my father. Amando and my grandfather had enemies. Amando recounted the heroic deeds of Edílio: the courage with which he and six soldiers defeated more than 300 rebels in the Battle of Uaicurapá. But other voices questioned this heroism, saying that in the 1839 Cabanos Revolt Edílio had presided over a massacre of unarmed *caboclos* and Indians. After this slaughter, he took possession of an immense area on the right bank of the Uaicurapá. One survivor must have carved the crimes of Lieutenant-Colonel Edílio Cordovil on the trunk of an ancient tree. Amando wanted to write a book, *The Deeds of a Bringer of Civilisation*, as an elegy to his father, one of the leaders of the counter-revolt. But he never wrote anything, as the freighters sapped all his energy and time.

I was left with very little money in Vila Bela, after paying for the pilot and the rental of the boat. The only way out was to sell the white palace, my last valuable property. I went into the Benchayas' pension and said: Salomito, I want to sell my palace, if you know of anyone interested . . .

Salomito thought this was just idle talk, or a sudden whim: words with no thought to back them up. But I insisted I was serious. He pointed his patriarch's beard at the table and said that Becassis was looking for a place to live and set up a little perfumery in Vila Bela. He was a courageous old man, determined to sell aromatic oils at a time when everywhere reeked of hunger and destruction, here and in Europe.

Becassis was sitting between Estrela and Azário, a strange boy. Estrela was a haughty woman, her long, curly hair touching the table edge. I observed her stiff body, her delicate hands, her shapely face, the glimmer behind her grey eyes. How I admired the foreigner's eyes. It was the second time I'd seen this woman; the first time I'd only seen her from a distance. She lived like a recluse, not wanting to flaunt her beauty. The old man noted that I was hypnotised by Estrela. I didn't yet know she was his daughter; Moroccan Jews and Arabs were reputed to be womanisers, and the older ones often married girls. This wasn't a husband's jealousy, but a father's. Becassis got up and asked about the house. I said, without exaggeration: It's the white mansion on Beira-Rio Avenue.

He introduced me to his daughter and grandson, and wanted to see the house straight away. The woman smiled, while the lad looked at me sideways, crossing his arms. I don't know if he mistrusted me. Or was it something I felt that distanced me from him? He didn't even say hello, and I paid no attention. That is, I registered Azário's impertinence in my memory and went with Becassis to the house.

The floor waxed by Florita was shining. What wasn't shining was the look in her eye. But my little flower kept her mouth shut. Becassis was impressed by the tall windows with their pointed arches, the large parlour, bedrooms and kitchen; he stopped to admire the crockery and the Portuguese tiles in the bathroom. Then we went round the garden, and I said that this was one of the few houses in Vila Bela with a decent cesspit. He looked at everything: the fruit trees, the stone fountain from my mother's time, the wooden pergola covered by a passion fruit vine. He tore a leaf from the climbing plant, rubbed it in his hands and smelt it. His voice faltered, as if it was someone else speaking, as he asked about the price.

Dr Estiliano, my lawyer, deals with that.

Even the price? asked Becassis.

The price above all.

Have you any other properties?

An area of the flood plain of the River Uaicurupá, I replied. The Boa Vida plantation.

Has it got plants with aromatic roots? The white resin tree, the black resin tree?

It's got everything, I lied. Then I said something true and of interest to me: It's even got a properly drawn-up contract.

Becassis's dry, hard face remained motionless. On the pavement, I gave him Estiliano's address and we parted.

Two weeks later, Estiliano informed me of Becassis's offer. Very strange. The buyer must have known I was going around with a begging bowl, for the price included the Boa Vida.

How did Becassis know it was for sale?

He found out from me, said Estiliano. You also mentioned the plantation and led him to understand that you were going to sell it.

It's a very low price for the two properties, I protested.

Becassis is the only one who can pay. He wants to sign two promissory notes that can be cashed in Belém. And he even agreed to pay your fare.

Without the two properties, I would have nothing left. There was Florita, whom I was supporting. I thought of a plan, and told no one. I couldn't . . . I agreed to Becassis's offer, and told the lawyer I would only sell the properties if Florita stayed in the white palace.

Do you want to sell the house and abandon Florita? asked Estiliano.

Abandon Florita? How could I abandon the interpreter of my dreams, the hands that prepared my food and washed, ironed, starched and perfumed my clothes? I'd been fond of her from the first moment I saw her in my room: the girl with the round face, full lips and smooth bowl-cut hair, the tender and sad look which acquired cunning and toughness living with Amando. Florita was jealous of me because I'd only slept with her once in the hammock: the game she'd taught me, saying: Do this, touch me here, squeeze my bum, don't do that, put your tongue here and lick me now: the game that was my farewell to my virgin youth, and which led to my punishment in the Saturno pension and the four or five years of Amando's contempt. I thought about all this and asked Estiliano:

Wasn't it my father, your friend, who brought Florita to work in the house?

In Amando Cordovil's house, not in a house of strangers.

I tried to convince Florita that when I came back from Belém I'd buy a house in the Santa Clara neighbourhood, where we'd live together. Becassis said that an employee from Salomito's pension was going to work in the house.

You'll have a family until I come back, I said to Florita.

She came up to me with a friendly look and tenderness in her eyes, brushed her lips across the back of my neck and licked my ear till I shivered. Then she whispered, with hatred:

You'll come back from Belém with the devil in your heart.

Becassis didn't hear the whispered words, but he saw my face yellow with fear. And my fear increased when I saw the stamp of an English bank on the promissory notes. I remembered the loan, the firm going bankrupt; my hands turned cold at the bad memory. Becassis questioned me apprehensively, as if I wasn't going to go through with the deal.

That's money, he said, pointing to the promissory notes.

The same bank, I said, thinking aloud.

But this time they're not going to take your money; this time they'll pay you, said Estiliano.

By chance I looked at Azário and grew irritated. Becassis reprimanded his grandson, who was pulling a devilish face. Estrela's face cheered me up. That woman's beauty didn't diminish my longing for Dinaura, but the idea of losing the white palace was disorienting me. Becassis seemed enthusiastic about buying the property. The matter-of-factness of our first encounter had gone. I'll not say the old man melted like butter, but he'd warmed up a bit; he was an honest buyer, and a vocal one. He even revealed the name of the perfumery: Tangier. He was going to buy the Bonplant perfumery and gather leaves and roots from the jungle at Boa Vida. He wanted to sell the scent of the forest to the whole of Brazil. If it worked, he'd export to Europe.

I put the notes in my pocket, imagining the flasks of aromatic oil at the back of the white palace. As I said goodbye to Estrela, I touched her delicate hand, then squeezed it, lingering, conveying infinite promise. And I forgot the widow's son, a strange boy, with a rigid body and hands too big for his age.

Estiliano and Florita couldn't understand my mood: I had just sold the last two properties and I wasn't depressed. Estiliano wanted to know what I was going to do afterwards.

Afterwards?

You've no longer got a floor or a roof for shelter.

I've got Florita. And a friend, who was my father's only friend.

He guessed that I was scheming something, and came to visit me in the last week I slept in the white palace, before I gave the keys to Becassis and embarked for Belém. He suggested that with the money from the sale I should buy two houses: one to live in and one to rent.

You're only half a step from poverty. I don't want to see a Cordovil living on the streets.

Then I decided to touch on a subject that I knew would cut him to the quick. I told him that in Boa Vida, after I'd rummaged through the papers in the

Mandarim box, I discovered that Amando Cordovil had been a smuggler and tax-evader. Was Estiliano aware of this?

He got up, and before he got to the door, I went on: it was the meat and Brazil nuts that Amando exported to Manaus. He took the cargo to other areas so as not to pay taxes in Vila Bela; then he unloaded everything on an island near Manaus and played the same trick. He bribed the customs official; he'd have bribed the devil himself.

The politicians blackmailed your father, said Estiliano.

They were his allies, his partners, I said. My father avoided duties and then shared the profits with them; then he helped the mayor's office, donated carts to collect the rubbish, gave the horses and oxen that pulled the carts, paid for the repairs at the slaughterhouse and the jail, even the jailers' wages. Then he did the same thing with the cargos for the barges and the *Eldorado*: he wrote to the governor of Amazonas, and to a civil servant in the Ministry of Public Transport. He died because he lost the competition for a big contract, just before the First World War: rubber and mahogany to Europe. His heart gave way, his greed was bigger than his life.

It wasn't greed, Estiliano burst out.

His loud voice gave Florita a fright. Even I was shocked by his outburst. Amando's sudden death had made him feel vulnerable. He'd had no time to burn the past away.

It wasn't greed, Estiliano repeated.

His red, sweaty face was shining; he couldn't move, suffering as he was from this episode of intemperance. The sweat ran off his chin and dripped to the floor. Amando was an ambitious man, he said, but an upright one. Florita knew that, everybody did. The farmers only thought about exporting meat to Manaus. Amando was the first one to sell cheap meat in Vila Bela. He wanted the people to eat, he wanted meat for everyone, but even for that he had to grease the politicians' palms. He wanted the jail to be clean, with food and bunkbeds. It wasn't greed. It must have been something else. Some people can die of greed, but not . . .

I never knew that man, I said brusquely. I read all the correspondence he received.

He never mentioned those letters to me, said Estiliano contemptuously.

Estiliano's blind loyalty to my father was getting on my nerves. Before he left, he warned me: Don't spend all the money, don't spend all that money in Belém.

Florita muttered that I shouldn't have sold the white palace; that I'd be sorry for the rest of my life.

Florita's mutterings didn't bother me. Without realizing it, I was being as stubborn and brutish as Amando Cordovil. I wanted to be different, but there was a shadow of my father inside me, like a stone inside a rotten fruit. I was determined to be the rind, to be thrown aside, and that way I'd do no harm to anyone.

The *Hildebrand* was due to dock in Vila Bela on a Saturday. On the Friday morning, I signed the documents in the registry office and handed the keys to Becassis. Then he said just what I wanted to hear most:

When you come back from Belém, I'll invite you to dine at home. My daughter will be pleased.

Buoyed by this I embraced Florita, expecting her to sob because she would miss me. But no. Not a single word.

I left everything in the house: the furniture, the crockery, the clock on the wall, even the linen sheets. The only thing I didn't leave behind was the memory of the time I had lived there.

The captain of the *Hildebrand* recognised my name. He remembered Amando's trips to Belém. He said I would travel in my father's favourite cabin.

He saw the surprise, perhaps even shock, on my face.

It's the only one that's not taken, he said.

I travelled where my father had slept. And the man's memory followed me downriver all the way to Belém. The only subject of conversation on board was disaster. It was like a boatload of survivors from a shipwreck. Near Breves I remembered the shipwreck of the *Eldorado*, and almost at the same moment I remembered a promise of Amando's. It was on the day he came back from a journey to Pará. He came into the white palace with a look of pleasure and triumph, and instead of talking about the freighters and the business, he mentioned the beauties of Belém: the Old Town, the Salt Quay, the Grande Hotel, the magnificent mansions, churches and squares. And the sea. The Amazon and the Atlantic, with their mingled waters. I wanted to see the city. He promised we'd go together on the next trip, but he went on his own. When he came back, he'd already forgotten the promise.

The Grande Hotel was a fabulous building. An old receptionist asked if I was a relative of Amando Cordovil. His son, I replied. He spoke feelingly of his guest's goodness and his tips, and asked how he was. Dead, I said.

Poor Doctor Cordovil, the old man said with sadness. He didn't tell me he had a son. He used to visit the tomb of a relative in the English Cemetery.

My grandfather's bones were buried in Vila Bela. I knew nothing of my grandmother, nor of any other relatives. Curiosity took me to the English

Cemetery. I walked around the little graveyard, reading epitaphs on Carrara marble gravestones. It was noon; hardly had I sat down on a stone seat than it began to rain. What the devil was I doing there? A face attracted my gaze. A portrait of a dead man. I went over to the stone: Cristóvão A. Cordovil, who died in a shipwreck on the coast of British Guiana. The name of the ship seemed tied to my destiny: *Eldorado*. The name, and the face of that Cordovil: angular, with a prominent chin and thick eyebrows. How could he be dead if he looked at me with the same look as my father? I was afraid of falling into a trap, of not getting the money from the promissory notes. I left the cemetery with this evil omen hanging over me. Amando was nowhere, but he seemed to be following my every step.

I went to the Grande Hotel to change and wait for the rain to pass. Then, in the English bank, I handed the manager the two promissory notes. He asked for proof of identity; I also handed him a letter that Becassis had written and signed, on

Estiliano's insistence. I was relieved when I had the packet of money in my hands, and I laughed at my own forebodings. I could taste the pleasure that Amando had always refused me. And I could spend it without a father or a guardian looking over my shoulder. I let my hair down in the Café da Paz and the bars of the Old Town; I met Mestre Chico and other bohemians and musicians who sang and played tunes and *modinhas* to the accompaniment of flute, guitar, violin and *cavaquinho*. I paid for the drink for these night time revels and the tickets to go to the operettas of the Chat Noir troupe in the Modern Theatre in Nazaré Square. We saw the dawn come up on the Salt Quay. Then I rented a launch and saw the sea for the first time. In the Paris n'América shop I bought pieces of Swiss organdie and French and Italian silk. They were presents for Estrela, Becassis's daughter, but it was as if they were for Dinaura. I cashed the second promissory note and bought clothes and shoes for myself and Florita; I went by the Alfacinha book-shop and got a box of French books for Estiliano.

I was sick of so much buying, spending, carousing, eating and drinking in the best restaurants. After more than two months of living that way, it felt like the same futile wasted life I led in Manaus, in the time before I met Dinaura. I couldn't forget her, and I had little hope of finding her.

In the hotel, I asked the old receptionist how much my father gave as a tip. It was a pittance. I'd give him twenty times that. I changed my mind when I opened my wallet: ten times would do, but in the end I gave him five pounds sterling. And lo and behold, the old man's face was wet with happiness. The news that I was a rich man with an open purse had the whole port in a fluster. And when the street vendors in the Ver-O-Peso Market offered me essence of Pará, I thought of the Tangier perfumery and of my meeting with Estrela. How could I marry her if I was all the time thinking of Dinaura? I went to Vila Bela with this doubt in my mind, and a little money. 'You'll come back with the devil in your heart.' Florita's words were more frightening than Estiliano's warnings. Because my little flower knew the two men in her life: me and my father. Estiliano only knew one side of my father, and with this one side he idealised the whole man and his soul.

Sometimes an omen is more powerful than reason, don't you think? A porter put all my luggage in a cart when I disembarked in Vila Bela. Before paying a visit to Estiliano, I decided to give the boxes with the pieces of cloth to Becassis's daughter. I remembered I'd bought nothing for Azário. That brat disturbed me. Something about him reminded me of my father. I decided to face Azário and accompanied the carter to the white palace. I went round the house to the end of the back yard, but there was no scent of oils and essences, no aroma. All there was was the smell of horse- and cow-shit. Where were the owners? The carter didn't know. And Florita?

She's out and about somewhere.

Go and find her.

It was strange to see the front of the house all boarded up. The Becassises must have gone to Boa

Vida, I thought. But when I saw Florita pushing a tray with wooden wheels, I realised she no longer lived in the white palace.

She told me that the perfumery was a lie. A week after I left, Becassis sold the two properties to the Adel family. The next day Florita had to leave the house. Estiliano rented a small room for her at the Santa Clara Harbour, and Leontino Byron gave her a tray to sell *beijus* and curd cheese.

Two friends of your father's saved me from the gutter, said Florita angrily. Even in death, he still helps me. And look what they've done to you.

I was on the bare earth of the street, between a cart full of boxes and a humiliated woman. I gave Florita the presents and said we could spend a few days in Estiliano's house. She put the packets on her tray and left without saying a word.

Stubbornness is stupid, it destroys our lives. I was flippant and stubborn to have ignored Florita's prophecy. This is what I was thinking as I walked towards the Francesa Lagoon. Estiliano was eating his lunch halfway along the table; around his plate were open books. He chewed, drank and paused to read one of the volumes. When he saw me, he put his spoon down and invited me to lunch. I refused and put the French books on the table; he smiled with pleasure. Becassis and Adel were clowns, I said, and I wanted to know what was behind their antics.

Why are they clowns? That's business. You know nothing of these things. Horadour Bonplant decided not to sell the perfumery. I even went to talk to him, but the Frenchman wanted a fortune. He put the price up each week, and so Becassis got fed up and decided to sell the two properties to Genesino Adel.

I don't believe that, I said to Estiliano.

Go by the perfumery and ask Bonplant your-self . . .

Amando, I interrupted. Where does he come into the story?

What do you mean?

Azário, Estrela's son. That sour young man, just like Amando. The same big hands, the same look as my father.

Fantasies, that's all you've got in your head, Arminto. Any money left in your pockets? Nothing left over, I bet? You've lost the white palace and the Boa Vida. You've lost everything.

He got up and walked round the table, shutting the books.

In times of prosperity it would just be a waste, said Estiliano. But in these poverty-struck times, it's suicide.

I stayed in the best hotel in Belém, tried to get the longing for Dinaura out of my system, threw money away as if there was no tomorrow. My father hadn't even mentioned me to the hotel receptionist. But I got my revenge . . .

Revenge? What is there after death? he asked. Now we're going to look for a house, the last place you'll live in.

With the money left over, I bought this shack. Genesino Adel didn't even give me back the furniture and personal objects from the white palace. He hated my grandfather. Only then did I find out that Edílio Cordovil had abused a Portuguese girl,

Genesino's mother, one of the many girlfriends Edílio abandoned. Salomito Benchaya told me this when I stopped by the bar in the Market for a drink. They say your grandfather got engaged, promised to marry, left the girl and went looking for another.

Amando must have done this with Becassis's daughter too. If Florita knew about it, she had decided to keep her mouth shut. The worst thing was her decision not to live with me any more. I had to learn to live without the flower of my infancy and childhood.

Sometimes, worried about my being on my own, Estiliano would come by for a chat. He didn't talk about his own life; there are people who die with their secrets. But one afternoon he revealed that he'd been very shaken by my father's death; and that the two of them had been planning a trip to Paris.

Just the two of you?

Yes.

On other visits, he commented on the books I'd bought in Belém. He said that the late afternoon inspired him and disturbed him, and at that time of the day he felt an absurd desire to suffer. He drank two bottles of red wine and, before it grew dark, he read poems by Cesário Verde and Manuel Bandeira. He left half drunk, his deep, hoarse voice intoning: 'Life passes, life passes, and youth will end . . .'

One Saturday afternoon he dragged me to a literary soirée at the Francesa Lagoon. Estiliano didn't let any of his books moulder on the shelves. When he moved here, he brought from Manaus a library that astonished the town. In the early mornings he walked down to the harbour of Santa Clara, returning to read. On Saturdays, he recited poems and offered wine and liqueurs to the few people in Santa Clara who read. He'd say: When I stop working, I want nothing more of laws and statutes, nothing at all. Just reading. I came out of the soirée missing Dinaura so much that I never went back. He showed me the book from which he'd copied the poem I sent to Mother Caminal, recited Brazilian and Portuguese poems, and some by a French poet, very modern, who'd written love poems while fighting in the First World War. These poems only gave more life to my desire for my beloved. When Estiliano finished reading, I said, hardly able to speak: This is torture.

That's our life when things go wrong, he corrected me. But the poets are the only ones who can speak of it.

For some time Estiliano carried on his visits, and in our conversations we avoided talking about Amando, the freighters, the past. He left books which I took a long time to read, because I'd stop at a page to think about Dinaura, or open at any page and my beloved would be there, disguised under another name, another life. I remember at that time he began to translate a Greek poem, and even gave me the first part of the translation. Then for a long time he didn't set foot here, after the rainy afternoon when he spoke of his beloved poets, declaiming their verses, while I looked at the river and cried while he was leafing through a book.

I've never seen you cry over a poem, Estiliano said.

Orphans of Eldorado

I'm not crying for the words. I'm crying because I long for a woman you hate. The Spanish Mother Superior lied to me . . . Someone lied to me.

He put the books in the leather briefcase, got up and said I should understand one thing: passions are as mysterious as nature. When someone dies or disappears, the written word is the only thing we have to hold on to.

I was going to send Estiliano to the devil; him, the written word, and all the poetry in the world, but the man was already out in the dirt street, and I was licking the tears from my lips. I never went to see him again, not even to ask for money. Some years later, when four tourists from São Paulo came by Vila Bela, I got a little money. Three women and a man—a writer. They were elegant poseurs, dressed all in black, and soaking wet from the heat. There was great excitement, and the men couldn't keep away from the socialites. The writer was striking up conversations with everyone: Indians, *caboclos*, artisans and popular composers. He never tired of recording the names of plants and animals. He ate everything, even fried piranha. The four of them were received by the mayor and honoured by the local council. In the dinner given by Genesino Adel, Estiliano was the only guest who knew something about the writer. The women were so impressed with the white palace that Estiliano told them about me and the Cordovils. The next day the *paulistas* came to visit me. So many people had gathered around the door, and even Florita came to see the tourists. I told them I'd inherited the white palace and now lived here. They asked to see the shack and left horrified by so much poverty. Then I showed them pieces of organdie and silk from the Paris n'América haberdashery. I wanted to sell everything, whatever the price. They bought it. One of them, the oldest, wanted to know who I was going to give such marvellous cloth to.

To my beloved Dinaura.

Has she died?

No, she's somewhere around, in some enchanted city. But one day she'll come back. If you hear that name, it's her, she's the only one in the world.

The three women looked at me as if I was a madman, and I got used to being looked at like that.

I gave part of the money to Florita and kept a little in case there was worse to come. Then I grew confused and lost count of the days, waiting for a miracle. My moods shifted: hope one day, despair the next. Those trees were planted by Florita. From time to time she'd bring some meat stew with *maxixe* and rice with *jambu* leaves soaked in *tucupi* sauce, delicacies she used to make in the white palace. She said I was crazy to think so much about Dinaura: she couldn't bear seeing me like this, gormless, with a face on me like a sad toad. She served my lunch, picked fruit from the garden, and when the bell rang five times, stayed close to me, to feel my anguish and see me so upset. Then she grumbled: So long ago, and you're still dreaming of that thankless woman. Then she went away, jealous and proud, pushing her tray. I never again gave her small change, nor did I ask for a penny. Now we were equals.

One morning when she was here, a boy came to

deliver a roll of paper. Genesino Adel sent it, he said.

I unrolled it, and saw a photo of my parents, just married. I tore the paper down the middle, gave Florita Amando's face, and put the picture of Angelina, my mother, on the wall of the only room in this shack. I waited two more years to enter the white palace. That was when Genesino Adel sold the building to the Justice Tribunal. I didn't visit the house; I went in by the back just to see the sculpted head of my mother in the middle of the fountain. I kissed the stone eyes, the face warmed by the sun, and asked the judge to authorise me to take the head to my room. He refused. Then I swore that never again would I set foot in the white palace. I looked at the stone head for the last time and asked my deceased mother to help me find Dinaura.

I bought a big canoe and moored in the harbour, offering trips to the passengers from the Booth Line. Then, when the *Hilary* opened the route between Liverpool and Manaus, I got fat tips. It was a huge ship, much bigger than those of the Hamburg–South

America line. On the canoe trips we saw egrets on the backs of buffalo, and sometimes a harpy eagle flying over a lake of black waters. I remember a group of tourists who wanted to see Indians. I said: All you need to do is look at the inhabitants of the town. But one of the tourists insisted: Pure Indians, naked ones. Then I took them to the Aldeia of my childhood and showed them the last survivors of a tribe. If you want to talk to them, I know an interpreter, I said, thinking of Florita. They didn't want to talk, just take photos. Then I asked them if they wanted to see the lepers on the island of Espírito Santo, and one of the tourists said no, a dry, definitive no. At the end of the trip I showed them the façade of the white palace, saying the house had belonged to my family. Then I recounted Dinaura's disappearance, but I think they didn't believe me, they thought I was mad. I was prevented from going into the restaurant and the public rooms of the *Hilary*, and the luxury of a whole era ended in a bitter memory.

One day, among the crowds getting off the boat,

while trying to convince an English couple to take a trip with me to the Macurany, I heard a high-pitched lament: Fresh *beiju* . . . Florita was shouting, as if the English understood Portuguese. She sold nothing. The English couple chose another boatman, and I lost my tip. As the *Hilary* whistled, the passengers waved goodbye and threw coins into the Indians' dugouts.

If I was younger, I'd leave this place, said Florita.

Where would you go?

To another world.

The ship's engines gave a roar, the smoke clouded the sky, and the canoes disappeared. The deserted harbour, the silent quays, left me feeling low. I looked at the ground and saw Florita's feet. Swollen, caked with dirt, her legs swollen too. I put my hands on her head and told her that my plan had been to marry Estrela only so as not to lose the white palace—a plan that wouldn't have worked because I loved Dinaura. But I hadn't suspected Becassis and Adel. Had she really thought they were going to trick me?

All I know is that everybody tricked me, said Florita.

She couldn't stand another day selling snacks for a pittance. Before, she was given bits of meat with bones in the slaughterhouse, but now, not even that. She put her hands on her back and murmured: My body's aching, Arminto.

I pushed the cart back here and we sat in the shade of the *jatobá*. We ate *beiju*, drank a bit of *tarubá* and recalled the nights of my childhood, when my father went round Manaus and Belém and Florita translated the stories we heard in the Aldeia. At the end of the afternoon, when we were walking along the bank of the Amazon, I thought about the woman: the *tapuia* who was going to live with her lover at the bottom of the river. I remembered the strange sky, with the rainbow that looked like a snake. Did Florita remember that afternoon?

She went into the water and, with her back to me, she said: That wasn't what she said.

But she was speaking in the *língua geral*, and you were translating.

I translated wrong, Arminto. It was all a lie.

A lie?

Was I going to tell a child that the woman wanted to die? She said that her husband and children had died of fever, and that she was going to die in the bottom of the river because she didn't want to suffer in the town any longer. The girls from the Carmo, the Indian girls, understood and ran away.

Only now you tell me. Why?

Now I feel what the woman was saying. That's why.

She got out of the water, climbed the side of the ravine and went to the Ribanceira. She collected the flowers of the *cuiarana* and sat in the very spot where I had had my only night of love with Dinaura.

You've had some days of happiness, she said, without looking at me. Does someone who's never had even that deserve to live?

Florita's voice wasn't recriminating, she didn't want to blame me. Nor was it threatening. I insisted she come to live with me, stop standing on her dignity.

And do you live alone? You live with a ghost.

Before she left, Florita gave me a river dolphin's eye. The left eye, for your desire, she said.

I thanked her and put it in my trouser pocket.

We met every time the *Hilary* docked, both of us trying to get a bit of money from the European passengers. When she saw me with Oyama, she left some *beijus* and left. The arrival of the Japanese brought life to the town; they built a settlement with Japanese houses at the edge of the Amazon, right at the mouth of the Ramos branch of the river. They founded other colonies on the Andirá River, on the lands of the *sateré-maués*, accomplished farmers. They planted rice, beans and maize, and even managed the great achievement of planting jute. Oyama stopped on the corner and, with a gesture, asked the name of the tree that gave so much shade, to which I replied *jatobá*. I gave him fruit from the garden and plant cuttings, and then we began to talk. That's to say: I didn't speak Japanese, nor did he speak Portuguese. He asked something and I said yes; I questioned him, and he laughed and shook his head. Sometimes I chattered on, and he made clicking sounds. In the end it was fine, because neither of us understood what the other was saying. Very friendly, Oyama was. He brought a fish prepared in the Japanese manner, and I stuffed myself. Then he bowed his head, said goodbye and never returned.

I stopped going to the harbour because lots of young people from Vila Bela were now boatmen and canoeists. They made a terrific racket to attract attention; then, by mimicry, they amused the passengers of the *Hilary* with their begging faces, and took the tourists off on canoe trips. I was getting too old and was redundant. So I withdrew from the world. I wanted silence. The only voice I wanted to hear was my own. That way, I could think of Dinaura's silence. Did the silence hide something obscure? Not a word, not a sound, this silence grew and seemed like a knife threatening me, cutting into my peace. Early in the morning, when the sun was still weak, I went out for a walk to the Ribanceira and leant on the tree trunk, the same *cuiarana* that

sheltered us that night of rain and pleasure. *Cuiarana*:
a tree with lovely flowers, thick petals, not in the
least pale: yellow, pink, almost red. The scent of the
flower is strong, as strong as a rose. And the fruit
is large and heavy like a man's head. When it falls
and lies forgotten on the ground, it smells like something rotten, something spoiled. Not even the pigs
will eat it. One late afternoon, during a downpour,
I lay down on the flowers and remembered that
night. And every year, in July, 16 July, the night of
the Patron Saint's Festival, I remembered the dance,
Dinaura's body whirling beside the dancer from the
Silêncio do Matá *quilombo*. Something had changed.
The festival ended at midnight, or even later. I heard
the voice of the penitents, the sounds made by the
musicians, other musicians, the laughter of women
piercing the darkness; I heard the noise of hurried,
furtive footsteps, I saw a moored boat rock back
and forth, then I heard other laughter with whis-
pers of pleasure. The delicious rapture of climax. I
shook with so much longing. On the morning of
17 July I thought of talking to Mother Caminal,

and on an impulse left here and crossed Sacred Heart of Jesus Square, where I saw the streamers from the festivities on the bandstand, bottles of *guaraná* and beer on the ground, the stage empty, the ashes of the bonfire; luckily, I didn't see Iro, the harbinger of bad omens. And that gave me hope. For a second I thought that I wasn't going to meet the headmistress, but Dinaura. I opened the door and saw a group of girls playing with a shuttlecock in the garden; something had changed, for these orphans were not working in the morning. I saw two nuns, the younger of them a novice. They were surprised by the presence of a man with sad eyes in his pale face, and dressed in old clothes. A middle-aged man who wanted to see the headmistress. Mother Caminal, I said. Our reverend Joana Caminal? She's in Spain, sir, said the novice. She left us six years ago. Our Reverend Mother wanted to die in Catalonia, but she is still alive. She didn't even say goodbye to me, I said resentfully. They looked at me uncomprehendingly. Then they moved away, took the orphans' hands, made a circle, sang and skipped. How lively they were. How much happiness in the house of God. Not a sign of my beloved. I came back here eaten up with a hellish longing. I dozed off after lunch, and woke to hear a voice asking me if it was really me in the rain, laughing or crying, with my hands full of flowers. A musician from the island even composed a tune, forgotten now: 'The Enchanted Woman'. The song told the story of Dinaura, and of her life as an unhappy queen at the bottom of the river. This was years ago, when I last walked through the town.

The sadness I felt that afternoon began mid-morning. I was picking pink *jambo* fruit when a man appeared. He was pushing Florita's tray very slowly, and stopped there at the side of the street. I went to see what he wanted and saw my Florita, my flower, lying on the tray.

Sleeping in the sun? I asked.

The man took his hat off and said: She died in the night.

He was a neighbour of Florita's.

She died quite suddenly, just like Amando. The

wake was in the chapel of the Carmo, out of respect for my father. I wept as if I were in front of my family's tomb. They were the last tears I ever shed. Florita's death broke the links with the past. I and I alone was the past and the present of the Cordovils. And I wanted no future for men of my kind. Everything will end in this old man's body.

On Sundays, Ulisses Tupi or Joaquim Roso left a fish there at the door. I salted and dried the steaks; that was my lunch, with lots of manioc flour to fill my belly, and a banana I picked in the garden. Is that the way I ended my life? Only that there was one more twist, which left me reeling. The Second World War reached this place. And for the first time a President of the Republic visited Vila Bela. The whole town went to applaud the man in Sacred Heart Square. Even the dead were there. I, who only lived for Dinaura, and could die for her, didn't leave this shack. President Vargas said that the allies needed our rubber, and that he and every Brazilian would do all they could to defeat the countries of the Axis. Then thousands of people from the Northeast went to work extracting rubber. Rubber soldiers. The freighters sailed the rivers of Amazonia again; they carried rubber to Manaus and Belém, and then flying boats took the cargo to the United States. The dreams and promises came back too. Paradise was here, in the Amazon region; that was what was said. What did exist, and I never forgot, was the ship *Paradise*. It moored just down there, at the edge of the ravine. It brought more than a hundred men from the rubber stands of the Madeira, almost all of them blinded by the smoke-curing of the rubber. There, where Aldeia was, the mayor ordered the forest to be knocked down so that shacks could be built. And another neighbourhood appeared: Cegos do Paraíso, the Blind Men of Paradise. Other rubber-tappers occupied the edge of the Francesa Lagoon and the River Macurany, and founded Palmares. And I didn't budge from here, still living under the same roof. I thought of the orphan when the flying boats flew over Vila Bela; I thought of life with Dinaura, in another place. I talked to her, imagining her by my side. And I announced out loud that I was going to meet her, and the two of us would leave this place. My imagination ran down the river as far as the sea, and that enlivened me. You see: a body still, with the imagination running loose, ideas full of excitement . . . That body survives. I copied the Greek poem translated by Estiliano, and read that poem so many times that I even memorised some lines: '*I'll go to another land, I'll go to another sea. I'll find a city better than this one. Wherever I cast my eyes, wherever I look, I see my life in black ruins here.*' I said these words looking at the river and the forest, thinking of the request I made to my mother, Angelina. Who else did I know? Cordovil was just a name with no memory attached. The older people of the town were dead and buried. Ulisses Tupi and Joaquim Roso were merely generous hands that left fish for my sustenance and went away. In the early morning I couldn't sleep. I heard the noise of the boats and jumped out of my hammock. They went by like ghosts in the night. I looked at the useless twinkle of the stars, drank, and sometimes slept right here, in the damp of the night air. And how many nightmares: endless shipwrecks. I awoke with images of boats colliding and crashing noises; I awoke with the image of Juvêncio's face, swollen and disfigured, with no eyes, his hands spread out, asking for alms. I spent the day fleeing from these things—unreal, absurd, they were, but they seemed so alive they frightened me. I didn't know what to do when I was awake, so I talked to myself to forget the nightmares. The fishermen and boatmen said I was off my head. And that rumour brought a visitor, my last and only friend.

It was some time since we'd seen each other. Neither of us ever went out. Estiliano sat right there, on that little bench given me by a *sateré-maué*. He was very old but still robust. And a little hunch-backed, his head inclined to the earth. He wore the same white jacket, with the emblem of the scales of Justice on the lapel. He believed.

We were silent for some time, until he said these words:

I'm going to die.

So are we all.

I'm going to die before you, he went on. What is it you're going around saying in town?

I no longer go to town, Estiliano. I say the same things without moving an inch. The Greek poem. Your translation of the Greek poet, the translation you never finished.

I repeated the words, looking at the Amazon and the islands.

He shook his head and sighed:

Useless words, Arminto.

Why useless?

Because, if you go away, you'll not find another town to live in. Even if you do, your own town will go after you. You'll roam the same streets until you come back here. Your life has been wasted in this corner of the world. And now it's too late, no boat will take you anywhere else. There is nowhere else.

Estiliano took from his jacket pocket an envelope with *guaraná* powder in it, the colour of blood. He put a little of the powder in his mouth, chewed and swallowed.

A life with Dinaura, I said. That's the only thing

that gives me courage. Dinaura had a secret to tell. She believed . . .

In this time of war, hunger and abandonment people believe in everything, said Estiliano. But Dinaura's secret . . .

He put the envelope into his pocket, slowly looking up at me with a tenderness I found embarrassing. Because it wasn't just tenderness—it was as if he was looking at my father. Then he said in a low voice: Dinaura came back to the island.

I got up and went towards him: Island? What do you mean?

He asked me to sit down and not get excited. He said he wanted to tell me before he died. It was a secret between him and my father. But he didn't know everything.

I know that Amando depended on connections with politicians, said Estiliano. He wagered everything on the bidding in 1912, and lost to a big shipping company. But that wasn't why he died. It's a long time ago, and you were still living in the Pension Saturno, and studying to get into the law faculty. Your father wanted to speak to me in the house in the Ingleses neighbourhood. He was nervous, worried. I hardly recognised the man. He said he was supporting an orphan girl. Out of pure charity. Then he said it wasn't just charity. And he asked me not to tell anyone. He didn't tell me if she was his daughter or his lover. At her age, she could have been either. At first, I thought she was his daughter, but then I changed my mind. I was never certain. It was the only time your father left me confused and hurt. He brought the girl here, said to Mother Caminal that she was his goddaughter and that she was to live with the Carmelites. She asked the headmistress to keep that secret. I know that Dinaura lived alone in a wooden house Amando built behind the church. She lived with privileges, good food, and I sent books because she liked reading. It was a mistake on Amando's part. A moral error. But he wanted to live here and be near her.

Dinaura, my sister? I said, choking.

Half-sister, Estiliano corrected me. Or step-mother. That's what I'm not sure about. That's why

I didn't want to tell you. I promised your father I'd look after her, if he died before me. To this day I don't know who she is. I discovered that her mother was born on an island in the Rio Negro. Dinaura wrote me a letter, asking to live there. She wanted to leave Vila Bela. When I came back from Belém, I spent two days here. You were in Manaus. It was at the time of the wreck of the *Eldorado*. I spoke to Mother Caminal and helped Dinaura.

We had one night of love, I said.

That's why she wanted to go away. In the same letter she said that your story only existed in novels.

Is she alive? Where is this island?

Estiliano opened a sheet of paper and showed me a map with two words on it: Manaus and Eldorado.

I read the words out loud and looked at Estiliano.

Once they were synonyms, he said. The colonisers confused Manaus or Manoa with Eldorado. They were looking for the gold of the New World in a submerged city called Manoa. That was the real enchanted city.

And the map? Is Dinaura in Manaus or on the island?

She went to live in the village on the island, Eldorado, said Estiliano. Someone, mistakenly or out of malice, told Mother Caminal that Dinaura was seriously ill. No, it wasn't your father. She might have got it into her own head that she was ill. She wouldn't tell me. I think only your father could drag any words out of that woman. Mother Caminal agreed to her leaving. And she went away. The island is a few hours away from Manaus. Dinaura must be in Eldorado. Alive or dead. I don't know. But I didn't want to die with that secret. That's why I've come here. Out of friendship for your father too.

My father. At that moment I thought: poor Estiliano, a senile old man. I told him I hadn't a penny to my name but I was determined to sell this shack to go to Manaus and the island.

He took a sheaf of notes from his pocket and put them on my knee. Good heavens: how long was it since I'd seen money! Then he said he was in a hurry, very busy with his own death. He smiled, without any warmth, and explained:

I have to go to the registrar's office to sign over my house and my books. I want to give everything to Vila Bela and realise one of my friend's dreams. Your father wanted to build a library in this poor town. He didn't live to do it.

He got up and embraced me. So that was the last time I saw Estiliano, wearing his white jacket, trousers with braces and old shoes.

Destiny is the most imponderable thing in life, he used to say. Stelios da Cunha Apóstolo. He died when I was on my way to Eldorado. He was buried in the Cordovils' tomb. I kept the Spanish poem, and to this day I have the map of the island.

I went in an old vessel: a steamship from the Mississippi, the last one to ply the Amazon. I hung round my neck the dolphin's eye Florita had given me and put my mother Angelina's photograph into my trouser pocket. I slept in a hammock in third class, on the deck level with the water. Lots of noise, birds and pigs tied up, a sour smell of sweat and dirt. The food was filthy. None of this mattered, because this could be the journey of my life, to the elusive heart of the woman I loved.

Very early in the morning, as the boat was nearing Manaus, I went up to the bridge to see the towers of the cathedral and the dome of the Opera House. I remembered the house in the Ingleses, the Pension Saturno and the Cosmopolitan Grocery, my jobs in the store run by the Portuguese and in the Manaus Harbour. In the Escadaria Harbour, a barge was unloading rubber. The smell made me nauseous, the balls piled up like a lot of dead vultures. An ugly vision, only a few blocks from the business I had inherited and lost. On the quay, I was surrounded by people selling objects left behind by the Americans during the Second World War. I bought nothing. No one recognised a Cordovil from the past. I might as well have been in the skin of one of the peddlers: the difference was our stories. But isn't that everything anyway? For vengeance or puerile pleasure I'd thrown away a fortune. But I'm not sorry.

I showed the map to an experienced pilot and

told him I was looking for a village on the island of Eldorado.

I know there's a leper town on one of the islands of the Anavilhanas, he said. Sick people who fled from the colony of Paricatuba.

Was that the sickness Dinaura was hiding? I imagined her beauty destroyed, and thought about the silence of our meetings. The pilot saw I was upset and asked if I felt dizzy. Angry was what I was. The question whether Dinaura was Amando's daughter or had been his lover was something that concerned only the two of them. And it would always remain a mystery. But wasn't I a part of this story too?

We left Manaus in a small launch, passing through the heart of the Anavilhanas archipelago in the mid-morning. The desire to see Dinaura made me lose my bearings. The desire, and the memories of Boa Vida. The sight of the Rio Negro defeated my desire to forget the Uaicurapá. And my childhood landscape lit my memory up, so long after. Ribs of white sand and stretches of beach contrasting with the dark water; lakes fringed by dense vegetation; enormous pools formed by the retreating waters, and islands that looked like mainland. Was it possible to find a woman in such a grandiose natural setting? By midday we reached the Anum branch of the river and sighted the island of Eldorado. The pilot tied the launch ropes to the trunk of a tree; then we looked for the trail marked on the map. The two-hour trek through the forest was painful and difficult. At the end of the track, we saw the lake of Eldorado. The water was bluish-black. And the surface was smooth and still like a mirror reflecting the night. It was unimaginably beautiful. There were a few wooden houses between the riverbank and the forest. Not a voice could be heard. No children—for in the most isolated settlements of the Amazon, children cannot be heard. The sounds of the birds only increased the silence. I thought I saw a face in a house with a straw roof. I knocked on the door— nothing. I went in and searched through the two rooms separated by a partition of about my height. A dark lump was trembling in a corner. I went over to it, crouched down and saw a nest of giant cockroaches. I felt stifled: the smell and the disgusting sight of the insects made me break out in a sweat. Outside was the immensity of the lake and the forest. And silence. This place, so beautiful, Eldorado, was inhabited by solitude. At the edge of the settlement we found a hut for making manioc flour. We heard some barking; the pilot pointed to a house in the shade of the forest trees. It was the only one with tiles, with a veranda protected by a wooden trellis, and a can with bromelias in it at the side of the steps. There was a noise. In the door I saw a girl's face and went towards her, alone. She hid her body, and I asked her if she lived there.

I live with my mother, she said, jutting out her lips in the direction of the other side of the lake.

Where are the others?

They've died and gone away.

Died and gone away?

She nodded. And slowly she appeared, until she showed her whole body, shrinking back with shyness and mistrust.

Do you work in this house?

I spend the day here.

Did she know a woman . . . Dinaura?

She recoiled a little, joined her hands, as if praying, and turned her head towards the inside of the house.

The room was small, with a few objects: a little table, two stools, a low shelf full of books. Two windows opened onto the Eldorado Lake. I stopped near a narrow corridor. Before I entered the room, the pilot and the girl looked at me, without understanding what was happening, or what was going to happen.

~

I returned to Vila Bela and remained hidden away here, but I was much more alive. No one else wanted to hear this story. That's why people think I live alone here, me and my madman's voice. Then you came in to rest in the shade of the *jatobá*, asked for water and had the patience to listen to an old man. It was a relief to purge this fire from my soul. Don't

we breathe through what we speak? Don't story-
telling and singing blot out our pain? So much I
tried to say to Dinaura, so many things she wasn't
able to hear from me. I wait for the tinamou to sing
at the end of the afternoon. Just listen to that song.
Then our night begins. You're looking at me as if
I was a liar. The same look as the others. Do you
think you've just spent hours in this shack listening
to legends?

Afterword

One Sunday in 1965, before there was TV in the Amazon region, my grandfather asked me to come and have lunch at his house in Manaus. I never refused these invitations, because I knew that, after eating the delicacies prepared by my grandmother, he would ask me to come and converse in the shade of a *jambeiro*. In reality, it was a monologue, which I interrupted only with questions. That afternoon, my grandfather told me one of the stories he'd heard in 1958, on one of his journeys to the interior of the region.

It was a love story, with a dramatic slant, as

happens almost always in literature, and, sometimes, in life. This story also evoked an Amazonian myth: the Enchanted City.

Many natives and dwellers on the banks of the Amazon believed—and still believe—that at the bottom of the river or lake there exists a rich, splendid city, a model of harmony and social justice, where people live as enchanted beings. They are seduced and taken to the bottom of the river by the inhabitants of the waters or the jungle (generally a river dolphin or an anaconda) and only return to our world with the mediation of a shaman, whose body or spirit has the power to go to the Enchanted City, talk to its inhabitants, and, perhaps, bring them back to our world.

I remember my grandfather spent some hours telling this story, and I listened entranced by his eloquence and his theatrical gestures.

Years later, when I read the accounts of the Amazon written by conquistadors and European travellers, I realised that the myth of Eldorado was one of the possible versions and variations of the

Enchanted City, which in the Amazon region is also called a *legend*. Myths which are part of the Indo-European inheritance, but which are also part of Amerindian culture and of many others. For myths, like cultures, travel and are interlinked. They belong to history and to collective memory.

I asked my grandfather where he had heard the story of the orphans. Years later, when I was travelling in the middle reaches of the Amazon, I looked for the narrator in the town he mentioned. He lived in the same house my grandfather had described, and was so old that he didn't know his own age. He refused to tell his story:

'I've already told it once, to a river trader who came this way and had the goodness to listen to me. Now my memory is very dim, it's lost its strength . . .'

Glossary

amapá: (*Hancornia amapa*) a tree with white wood and which exudes a white gum used in medicine.

beiju: a light ball made of toasted manioc flour, often sold in packets in the streets.

Booth Line: the main steamship line plying between Liverpool, Portugal, Madeira, the Azores, and up the Amazon to Belém, Manaus, and as far as Iquitos in Peru.

caboclo: a person of mixed indigenous and European descent.

Cabanos Revolt (1835–1840): Also known as the Cabanagem, this was a violent revolt against the political elite of Pará, notable for being almost exclusively supported by the poor and the indigenous population.

cavaquinho: a small guitar, similar to a ukelele, very widespread in Brazil and used in folk ensembles.

Cesário Verde (1855–1886): One of the most important and individual Portuguese poets of the nineteenth century, the first to free himself of romantic sentimentality and move towards a realism influenced by Baudelaire.

cuiarana: large tree (*Buchenaria grandis*) with red flowers and inedible fruit the size and colour of olives.

farofa: a dish made of manioc flour, fried with pieces of egg, meat etc. It is often used as a stuffing.

guaraná: a climbing plant (*Paullinia cupana*) native

to the Amazon, whose fruit is used to make a fizzy drink very popular throughout Brazil. See *sateré-maué* below.

jaçanã: a water bird (*Jacana spinosa*) similar to rails and moorhens, with long toes allowing it to walk on floating plants.

jambeiro, jambo: a tree of Asian origin (*Eugenia jambos*), with pink fruit (*jambo*), known in English as rose apple.

jambu: a herb of the Compositae (*Wulffia stenoglossa*), with yellow flowers. Its leaves are eaten boiled and used to flavour rice.

jatobá: a tree of the Leguminosae (*Hymenaea courbaril*) found throughout much of Brazil, and exploited for its wood.

língua geral: a language of indigenous, Tupi origin, though with European influence, and much used as a lingua franca in the Brazilian past, and in the Amazonian region. It is also sometimes called *nheengatu*.

Manaus Harbour: originally the name of the (British) company which administered the Port of Manaus; the name came to signify the whole port area of the city, with its warehouses, docks etc.

Manuel Bandeira (1886–1968): One of greatest poets of Brazilian modernism, and one of the oldest. His poems are often short and sharp, combining strong feeling (often about death—the poet suffered from tuberculosis) and ironic control.

maxixe: a common low-growing plant (*Cucumis anguria*) with small, green, spiny fruit, much used for cooking.

modinha: a traditional form of popular song, usually sentimental in tone and in the minor key.

paricá: a tree of the genus *Anadenanthera*, with white flowers. Its leaves, seeds and bark are used to produce a powerful powder or snuff, whose use in the Amazon is restricted to shamans. It is reputed to give them curing powers, and produces visions.

paulista: name given to people from the state and the city of São Paulo, the largest in Brazil, and the centre of the country's wealth and industry.

President Getúlio Vargas (1882–1954): Vargas came to the Brazilian presidency in the 'October Revolution' of 1930, and kept in power by increasingly dictatorial means until 1945. His regime had fascist aspects, and he had good relations with the Axis powers. However, he eventually yielded to American pressure and joined the Allies—part of the motivation for this was the renewed importance of Brazilian (Amazonian) rubber, now that Malaya had fallen to Japan. He returned to the presidency in 1951, and after being implicated in the attempted murder of his rival Carlos Lacerda, committed suicide on 24 August 1954.

quilombo: a settlement of runaway slaves, of which there were many throughout the colonial period and the nineteenth century.

sateré-maué: an indigenous group inhabiting the middle reaches of the Amazon. They were the first group to cultivate *guaraná* (q.v.), a fact to which they give great importance. In their myths, they attribute their origins as a group to this discovery.

seu: an untranslatable way of referring to someone with familiarity, but also with a certain respect— *seu* Pedro, for example—the word is a corruption of the more formal 'senhor'.

tapuia: a word originally applied to indigenous groups who spoke languages not belonging to the large and important Tupi group. In the novel, it is used to mean an indigenous person who, through subjection to white people, has lost part of his or her own culture.

tarubá: an alcoholic drink of indigenous origin made from fermented manioc.

tucupi: a condiment made of pepper and manioc juice purified over a fire to the consistency of molasses.

tupinambá: name given to several tribes who speak or spoke tupi-guarani, the most widely distributed indigenous language in Brazil.

urucum: a small tree (*Bixa orellana*) with a fruit whose red or yellow juice is used as a colourant in food, and by indigenous groups for body painting.

Acknowledgements

I have freely used a few indigenous narratives and passages about myths of the Brazilian Amazon from the books of Betty Mindlin, Candace Slater and Robin M. Wright. Although this fiction does not directly refer to the Indians or to indigenous culture, my reading of the essay *A inconstância da alma selvagem* ('The inconstancy of the savage soul'), by Eduardo Viveiros de Castro, was important for the under-standing of the *tupinambá* peoples of the Amazon, and as an aid to reflecting on this novel.

My thanks to Jamie Byng, director of Canongate, who interested himself in the project for this book and included it in the Myths collection. Special thanks to Ruth Lanna, Samuel Titan Jr. and to my friends and publishers Luiz Schwarcz, Maria Emília Bender and Márcia Copola, who, as always, provided me with excellent suggestions.

Other friends who read the originals know how grateful I am for their patient, dedicated readings.